THE JEKYLL AND HER HYDES

USA TODAY BESTSELLING AUTHOR

SIERRA ROWAN

Proofreading: Happy Ever Author and Editing by Kimberly

Cover Design: Cover Design by Jervy

eBook ISBN: 978-1-955991-26-1
Paperback ISBN: 978-1-955991-19-3

Originally published as the short story "The Jekyll and Her Hydes" in the Crimson Vendetta Anthology

First published as standalone edition: July 2024
Urbana, IL, USA

v.0.1

AUTHOR'S NOTE

If you would like content guidance, please see the
author's website at sierrarowan.com.

ICE CREAM
Cookies
CANDY
Candy
Tasty
sing along

CHAPTER 1

CREEPY MABEL

They call me Creepy Mabel.
I'm such an awful sight.
And if you're acting naughty,
you will not last the night.

Ten steps to the stairs. Twenty to the door. Three to the corpse on the concrete floor.

I grin as I sway back and forth to the music of Mardi Gras coming from the streets outside. It's party night again here in the city. People in funny masks dancing and laughing everywhere you go.

I like to laugh.

I don't wear a mask.

Well, besides the *other*, but then, she would say that about me.

I'm no mask.

The corpse gurgles.

I stop swaying. I bend at the waist, my hands clasped behind my back like the teachers used to do when they were getting our attention as we played on the floor in preschool. They weren't fun, though. They talked like we weren't both there. They made us sit at a table and smile pretty.

They didn't like it when I made the bad principal scream.

I cock my head to the side, sending my dark hair swaying. He's an interesting corpse, in a way. Well, an interesting not-*yet* corpse, but that part will happen soon. He carried a special keychain, for one. All twisty and shiny like brass. And he has freckles on his cheek that form the shape of the other's favorite constellation, Libra. His brown hair was made of boingy curls before his blood turned them into a mop, and he has three earrings in his left ear and none in his right. Tattoos of roses cover his left arm, but there's only plain tan skin on the other. Keeping the sides of himself apart, maybe.

Silly.

But in every other respect, he's the same as any other soon-to-be corpse. He has keys for a rental car on his twisty little keychain. He stayed in a hotel that takes cash, not card. He knew what he wanted, and he'd had a plan—to find somebody at the party, have fun in his special way, and then return to his life of boingy curls and triple earrings, where maybe he'd get a brand-new tattoo.

And same as every time before, he thought no one would ever know a thing.

But I knew. I saw him in the alley. I heard the scream past the music, past the party, and I heard the struggles and the cries. Figures twisted around him, ghostly and half lost to the dark, wailing in voices no one else could hear. They sobbed because they were his roses, each as unable to stop him in death as they had been in life.

But that's why they have me.

I am the vengeance and I am the blood, the one to whom dead souls cry.

I am the one who lives in the dark, born to set the wrong things right.

Slinking along the wall, lost in the shadows and the garbage and the stink, I stalked him and he never saw me coming. The dead did. The dead always do. Not all the dead are tied to those who killed them, but sometimes they linger out of pain or rage or because they're trapped until justice can be done. Their wails grew louder at the sight of me, begging me to act, begging me to stop him from adding her to their number.

The other tries to give them a different kind of vengeance. She calls police and talks to lawyers. She seeks justice from the living on behalf of the dead.

I am not as patient as her.

I act now.

When I rose up behind him, the one he'd made his prey spotted me first. She was pressed to the brick wall, her cheek bloody from where he'd hit her. The horror in her eyes when she saw me was unavoidable.

His horror was candy.

At first, he blustered. He spat out curses and slashed at me with his blade even as his grip on his prey faltered and let her slip away. But when his silly little weapon didn't work on me, he retreated instead, puffing himself up with arrogance like he could scare me, right before he tried to run.

They always try to run.

"Please..." he whispers from where he lies on the ground.

"Beg me, beg me, says the judge's man. Beg me, beg me while you can."

His bloodshot eyes widen like he's latched onto something hopeful. "Please. Please, I'll give you anything you want. Please just don't—"

I bend closer. My lips pull back as I smile. His horror rises again, flickering past his hope as he stares at me. I see my face reflected in his terrified bloodshot gaze.

Teeth stained black. Large orange-ringed eyes. Skin green and mottled like the pretty lichen that grows on a tree. My dark hair hangs like a curtain around my face, long and stringy just how I like it. The other one wears hers pink and bright like she's trying to balance us out, and she never lets her green eyes bulge like mine.

She's worried by me, the other is. She lets darkness take her when I come, and she hides in her life of light when I leave.

I scare her.

That can't be my focus, though. Not right now. Not when there's work to be done.

"But did they scream?" I whisper to him. "Did they beg? And did you listen, or did you just make them dead?"

My knife takes his throat in a single slice.

Blood sprays the concrete floor. I flicker away just long enough to avoid a single drop. The other would be upset if we became coated in blood spatter.

She's so picky about such things.

The dead cry out, descending upon him as his soul escapes his body. They won't hold him for long. Just enough to return their pain. Just enough to give it to the one who dealt it, and who will bear it from now on.

Light spreads above them, emanating stronger and stronger from the single bulb hanging in the room. The glow is bright like the sun and soft like the moon. It washes away the pretty moldy walls and the sweet mildew of decay. There is only the glow and the sense of voices just beyond hearing, calling come see, come see.

The peaceful dead melt into it. Below them, his soul writhes, seeing the light, unable to reach it. Held down by what he did and wailing as all his victims float into a glow that slowly fades.

Darkness rises from the shadows in the corners of the room now. His soul thrashes harder. He screams as the deepest darkness has its way.

And then all the dead are gone.

Mold and mildew return and the only light is the glow of the single bulb above me, dim as a candle and flickering from its old wiring. Laughter and song carry from the street.

I look down at the body and smile.

"Waste not, want not, so they say. It's time for Creepy Mabel to sit down and play. So from the tip of your toes to the top of your head, you'll serve a new purpose, now that you're dead."

CHAPTER 2
MABEL

I open my eyes and groan. My mouth tastes nasty. I'm still in my clothes from last night. And the clock on the wall says it's half past two in the afternoon.

Dammit.

For a moment, I lie in bed, as if my pillows and blankets can delay the inevitable. Sunlight streams past the gauzy curtains and tall windows of my bedroom. Faint sounds come from the street outside, but they're fairly calm despite the fact Mardi Gras is going on. My family chose this quiet street generations ago, and thankfully it hasn't gotten so gentrified in the years since that tourists find it particularly interesting.

Nope, nothing here to draw attention, and just

enough privacy that we never have to worry about nosy neighbors spotting... well, anything.

Doesn't mean I don't have to be careful though.

I sit up and scrub a hand over my face—checking first that it's not covered in anything gross. "Okay, Creepy, what'd you do?"

The sensation of a chuckle and a grin from deep inside my mind is the only answer.

But it's enough.

"Just tell me you didn't kill whoever it was here in the house."

A dry, offended feeling comes up, so strong my own eyebrow twitches as if it wants to arch at the question.

"Oh, please. Like you haven't made that mistake before."

Bulging eyes narrow. She doesn't like to be reminded of the times she's messed up.

I sigh. "Fine. Could you at least try brushing our teeth before we pass out next time?"

A glower. She hates toothpaste, no matter what flavor I buy. It's not like it does much for her teeth anyway.

I roll my eyes and swing my legs out of bed. There aren't any blood spots where I can see, but I'll run the UV light over this place later just to be sure.

Ah, the joys of life as a Jekyll.

Over the centuries, supernatural scholars have held plenty of theories as to what we are. Our Jekyll sides look human—regular skin, regular eyes, teeth that have seen a dentist in our lifetimes—while it's really just a free-for-all with the Hydes. Because of the Hydes, though, scholars lump us in with monsters, even if it's a rough connection at best. Gargoyles, wraiths, and so on aren't the same as us on multiple levels, not the least of which is that they *know* they don't come from this world. We're fairly certain we do, though since our origins are murky, we can't be one hundred percent sure.

But throughout history, there've been theories about us, practically one for every age. In ancient times, some people called us children of Janus, the god with two faces. Others said we were connected to Hathor, the Egyptian goddess of multiple forms, or Kali, the Indian goddess with several aspects. Then Christianity came along and colonized whole chunks of the world, and in those places, we were suddenly considered souls possessed by Satan, in need of exorcism or—when that failed—death to save us.

Not fun.

Robert Louis Stevenson ambled in several

centuries later, writing the book that gave us our current names, though he got more than a few details wrong. Eventually, modern medicine jumped on the "explain us" train, with supernatural doctors trying to say we were byproducts of radiation or shapeshifter twins conjoined in unusual ways. Then came psychology, which our Hydes never really trusted. It didn't get any easier when those professionals claimed the Hydes were really just suppressed emotions or figments of our imagination that we could be counseled or medicated out of possessing, because they actually only existed in our minds.

Yeah, folks didn't hang on to that theory for long—and not just because the Hydes liked to prove their existence by eating the ones espousing it.

But as much as I know the rest of the supernatural world would like a way to explain our kind, the reality is, it doesn't much matter. We may not have legends telling where we came from like the wolf shifters do, or ancient origin stories like the vampires claim, but we have a calling and our Hydes do too.

Though in their case, it's one that tastes awful and sometimes gets a bit messy.

A hot shower and a visit with my toothbrush later, I'm feeling enough like myself to face what remains of the day and so I head for the stairs. There are three other doors in the hall on this level, and four more on the next floor down. They're all closed, same as they always are unless some of my associates are passing through and need a place to stay.

In their circles—the circles of the underground that save supernaturals from being the victims of predatory humans called traders—this house is code-named La Fleur, and it offers a place for all kinds of people to hide.

But right now, my home is so empty, so quiet, that the high ceiling makes my footsteps echo and I can hear every creak of the old wooden floor as I walk.

The sounds are all familiar and comforting in their way, as are the smells of herbs and flowers that carry from the ground floor and give the house its code name. I hang those everywhere, partly for use in the magical spells I concoct for clients and partly for comfort. Just one more way to ground myself back in who I am. What I'm doing.

The life I've built in my family home, even if I'm the only one left here.

Creepy glowers at me again from the darkness of my mind. She doesn't like to be reminded of that either.

The fact we're alone.

I exhale sharply, reminding her it's for the best. Mom and Dad passed away years ago, and as far as family is concerned, that just leaves Auntie, who lives in the Appalachian Mountains so she can protect the locals there, and Uncle—her brother—who lives out in the Pacific Northwest for the same reason. And yeah, there used to be more of us. People who weren't my relatives. Other families my parents mentioned from time to time. But life saw fit to fuck that up too, and since I never met any of those folks and they've never tried to come visit, by this point I'm guessing none of them are still alive.

Add to that the fact we can't just tell what one another is on sight—as Jekylls, we look the same as any other human on the street—and that means Creepy and I haven't laid eyes on one of own kind in years.

Truth is, there just aren't enough of us anymore, so the ones who are left spread out and help where we can. And besides, we're doing fine on our own.

If we don't get too close to anyone, we can't really lose anyone else, now can we?

She mumbles unhappily in my mind, but she doesn't argue. She knows I'm right.

I push open the swinging kitchen door and freeze. "Oh, for the gods' sakes, Creepy. Are you *kidding* me?"

A foot sticks halfway out of the stew pot. Another rests on the butcher block. There's gnaw marks on the ankles and a big black garbage bag tied up in the corner. I don't have to guess what's inside.

She's been busy.

"Dammit, you don't bring bodies here either! You —" I spot his keys on the counter beside my jars of spices. My heart sinks at the twisted symbol on his keychain. "Oh, fuck."

A trader.

I squeeze my eyes shut, muttering more curses to myself. But I know what Creepy must've thought. That this is fair. A twisted form of justice, even. After all, traders sell bits of supernaturals at their secret markets—when they aren't throwing supernatural kids into cages to fight, selling them as pets, or grinding up the adults' organs for powders, anyway. So why not return the favor?

"We don't do blood magic, you idiot. Or sell bits for it either. And this... Dammit, this is how we end up in a cage too."

She recoils in my mind. She doesn't like cages.

"Yeah, exactly." I scowl, but even without her watching me, I know my expression is half-hearted.

"How'd you find him? Was he hauling in a shipment of supernatural kids or what?"

Images pelt me, hard and fast like I've pissed her off. I cringe back from the onslaught, one hand catching on the counter and bracing me.

It takes a minute for me to find my voice again. "We could have called the cops. Stopped him and then tried to get the woman to press charges."

Now I'm the idiot as far as she's concerned.

"Fine. But he's a trader. If he operates with any kind of crew, they're bound to come looking for him."

I can feel her grinning like that's a good thing.

"*Cage*, remember? This shit is a real quick way to get locked up, and then you don't get to stop the bad ones ever again."

She sulks at that, like it's my fault the criminal justice system doesn't look more favorably on vigilantes.

But then, that's hardly the only problem. Your average human cop or FBI agent doesn't have a clue we exist. Even that damned secret organization known as the Government-Sanctioned Slayers—a.k.a. the GSS—seems to think we're just a myth.

It *really* needs to stay that way.

"Look, just stop bringing bodies home. This is a safe house, remember? It's not helpful. And if you do that for me, then..." I rack my brain for the bargaining chip least likely to get me arrested. "We can go play with the gators this weekend, all right?"

She grins so wide, it makes my lip flinch.

I exhale, trying to ease her back gently. "Good. It's a deal. So now just stay put, don't fuss, and don't interfere, okay?" I head for the closet where my disposable gloves and bleach are stored. "I'll get rid of the body."

ONE OF THE FIRST THINGS YOU LEARN AS A YOUNG JEKYLL IS how to clean up after your Hyde. It's right up there with tying your shoelaces on the list of life skills Jekyll parents teach their children. So by the time sunset rolls around, no one would ever know my kitchen recently played host to an impromptu episode of *Dexter* or that my specially designed furnace burns so hot because it just made dust out of a body.

But gods, it's exhausting.

It's past sunset by the time I finish, and as I'm packing up the last of my cleaning supplies, my phone rings.

"Men suck," my friend Tamira says before I can

even say hello. "You still coming out for drinks tonight?"

I laugh. "I take it things didn't work out with Mr. Tall, Dark, and Tiger Shifter?"

"Is it a red flag when he's more interested in asking about your family pedigree than whether you're okay after you got food poisoning on your last date?"

I tuck the bleach back into the closet. "Pretty sure it is, yeah."

She sighs. "Why are all the good supernatural guys taken?"

I chuckle. "Oh, I've got no answer to that."

Truth is, I've tried a few dates with non-Jekylls and even had a handful of relationships with supernaturals that lasted maybe a few months or even upwards of a year. But while shifters or vampires can understand being supernatural, and some can even understand having a side of you that isn't quite *sane*, it's still hard to explain to someone else what it's like to have a Hyde.

To say nothing of what it's like for any potential partners to live with one.

But whatever Jekylls are still out there are scattered around the world. We don't have meetups or annual conventions, and for our own safety, we never mention what we are on the internet, not even in code.

The Government-Sanctioned Slayers have eyes every-where, and even in the supernatural world, bigotry is real. But that much distance and silence doesn't leave a lot of opportunity for dating among my kind—or even knowing each other exists.

Meaning I've never laid eyes on a Jekyll guy, much less had the chance to date one.

"Well, whatever, right?" Tamira rallies. "His loss. See you at Final Toast in twenty?"

Creepy does a little dance in my head. She loves that bar. The owner really leaned into the whole "death" vibe with dark walls, flickering lights, and eerie decor reminiscent of a gothic horror aesthetic from the Victorian age. The bar is located in an old mortuary not far from one of New Orleans' many cemeteries, and even if it's technically a human estab-lishment, it's still a favorite hangout for a number of the supernaturals in the area. I hear the vampires even have a tourism guidebook that suggests it.

"Yup."

I hang up and glance around the kitchen, checking for anything left to do, but there's nothing.

Nobody cleans like a Jekyll.

My eyes land on the drawer in the kitchen island where I hid the trader's keychain, and my skin crawls. I called my contacts while I was cleaning, warning them about what Creepy and I found. They're going to keep an eye out, same as ever, and everyone will do their best to spot any of the traders' potential secret markets that might crop up. But there's every possibility he wasn't here on "business" this weekend—at least, not the *capturing supernaturals* kind—and without a trail to follow or evidence of other traders in the area, there isn't much more to be done.

The whole situation means Tamira isn't the only one who could use a drink right now.

Nineteen minutes later, I've changed into a short emerald dress that goes well with the pink streaks in my hair; I've got on my strappy black sandals that I've worn enough times to know they won't give me blisters, and I'm walking through the door of Final Toast.

"Oh my God, Mabel." Tamira comes rushing up to me. She's wearing a sleek gold dress that ends at mid-thigh and tall black boots that hug her calves tightly. Her dark hair is pulled up in a collection of intricate braids tonight, fastened by a glistening hair clip I'm pretty sure I lent her ages ago, and her amber skin is dusted with gold powder on her sharp cheekbones. She looks every bit the gorgeous hyena shifter she is, underneath the human disguise.

Hyena shifters are like Jekylls in their way. Misunderstood. Assumed to be one thing when really, they're quite another. Yes, the hyena side can be vicious, same as a Hyde. Yes, there are stories of people who've lost control, who've become monsters in more than just title. There's always a danger when you live with a predator inside you that someday it will snap.

But in reality, that's an issue for any species, even humans. They may not have the same force inside them that we do, but it's still a risk. And regardless, we're more than that. Hyena shifters and Jekylls can be loyal and protective of friends and strangers alike, and we know more than many people do about seeing the world from the outside. I think it's part of why Tamira and I have been friends ever since her parents came to New Orleans looking for mine because they needed a magical specialist to help their daughter balance out those sides.

"What's wrong?" I ask her, but she just grins.

"You have to come see these guys."

My brow climbs. "That's fast, even for you."

She throws me a half-heartedly dirty look, but it's ruined by the grin hovering around her lips. "Trust me."

Taking my hand, she pulls me with her through the crowds that are already gathering inside Final Toast. There's a local band playing here later tonight, and from the looks of it, they're getting popular enough to draw more than just the locals.

Creepy stirs in my mind, making my heart pick up speed. She just got done with a kill. She should have been placated, at least for a time.

But right now, she just feels... eager.

"Chill," I murmur.

"Did you say something?" Tamira asks, glancing back.

I shake my head.

She returns to leading me through the crowd.

I exhale, annoyed at Creepy. I know she likes the bar, but this feels different.

She's suddenly *really* awake and she's not giving me the slightest clue as to why.

"Okay, so..." Tamira slows in front of a table near the far wall. "Guys, this is Mabel, the one I was telling you about."

She steps aside and pulls me up next to her, and suddenly, it's all I can do to keep Creepy from shoving her way to the forefront and shifting us in front of all these humans and the three drop-dead hotties at the table.

"Mabel." Tamira flashes me a grin. "Meet Huck, Phineas, and... Zeb, was it?"

The one called Zeb nods, smiling this calm,

smooth smile that just oozes confident sexuality. He's got golden-tan skin, dark hair that brushes his shoulders, and these pitch-black eyes that just pin me, making a tingling chill rush over my skin straight to my breasts and a nervous tangle of heat spin in my middle before it sinks lower.

I fight to give no sign of how his mere presence is affecting me, and gods help me, I wish I hated what it was doing. Or better yet that I wasn't reacting like this at all, because I'm not a fan of anything that means my body is not fully under my control.

Except I'm already turned on, and this guy hasn't even opened his mouth to say hello.

I tear my gaze away from him, but it doesn't help. His friends aren't an improvement. Zeb's got his arm looped casually over the shoulders of the guy to his left, the one with damn near colorless skin and short ice-white hair that transitions to electric blue on the tips. The short spiky hair only serves to set off his sharp jaw and eerily light eyes, the latter of which haven't left me for a heartbeat. From the way Tamira introduced him, I'm guessing he's Huck.

And that leaves Phineas, the strong, dark god of a man leaning back against the booth seat cushions. He's nothing but muscle, that much I can tell through his tight black t-shirt, and his face has this considering air, like he's already weighed everything about me but wants to know more. His eyes are calm as night and yet mesmerizing as hell. He's got long braids all tied back at the nape of his neck, and there's some kind of tattoo on the side of his throat that I can't make out against his dark brown skin.

Not that I'm looking.

But, gods, Creepy likes the sight of them. She's practically salivating at the thought of touching them, getting to know them, and coming out to say hi.

Which is number one on my list of Bad Plans right now, so it only takes a second before I'm pulling Tamira back with me while looking anywhere but at the guys as I try to get my Hyde under control.

"What's this about?" I demand of Tamira. "Do you know these guys?"

She shakes her head. "Just met them. But come on…" She chuckles, twitching her head back toward them. "There's three. One for each of us and maybe one to share."

Yeah, no. Not happening, and not just because Creepy is now snarling at the thought of anyone touching them but us.

Which is madness.

But these guys have *dangerous as fuck* written all over them in big neon letters I'm amazed Tamira can't see. Down underneath their casual postures and their relaxed expressions, they're killers. It's in their eyes.

I should know. I see the same thing every time I look in the mirror.

"So, Mabel…" comes a smooth voice that I like the sound of just a *little* too much, especially when he's saying my name.

My eyes dart back. Zeb. That was Zeb.

Not that it matters.

"Your friend says your family's been in the area for a while. I bet you'd make a great tour guide."

I throw Tamira a small glare and murmur under my breath so quietly only a shifter would hear. "You were telling them about me?"

She shrugs, still grinning, and murmurs back, "They smell good. There's something… I don't know, *magic* about them."

Supernaturals, then. Maybe. But supernaturals with something hellaciously wrong about them that's setting me on edge and making Creepy drool.

Which makes no sense.

Creepy doesn't like that I'm not smiling back at the guys, though. Hell, she doesn't like that I'm not climbing over the table to lick them like lollipops.

What the hell is her problem?

Could they be like me?

The thought stops me cold, leaving me tangled between caution, fear, and longing. Jekylls are the freaks of the supernatural world in our own way. Even when I've gone on dates, I've waited a good long while before revealing what I am. It took me years before I'd even tell Tamira more than the most basic of details about my life.

Secrecy is the best way I can protect Creepy. And myself.

Because even if these guys are supernaturals, that doesn't automatically mean I'm safe. What if they're double agents for the GSS? Or witches, for that matter? Jekylls might be somewhere in the gray area between humanlike and monster, but the witches have a big issue with monsters in general, and they sure as hell don't like Jekylls practicing magic. I've stayed off the shit list of the Grand Coven and others like them, but that doesn't mean some random group of witch guys won't hassle me if they find out what I am.

"Do you know any fun places to eat around here?" asks the icy-haired one, Huck, in a sweet, kind voice that slides around me like a hug and only adds to the way my insides are melting for no goddamn reason.

Creepy pushes at me harder. My hand shakes. I can feel my fingertips shifting.

Fuck.

I can't stop the way she spasms my lips into a smile, and I can feel her protest when I take a step back from the table. I don't know what the hell is wrong with her, or me, or why she's acting like this. But holy shit, she's about to make me lose control in the middle of a crowded bar, in front of three hot strangers and the gods know who else. "I-I'm sorry. I need to go."

I turn and bolt through the crowd for the door.

CHAPTER 3
MABEL

The air outside the bar feels about a thousand degrees cooler, but that's probably only because of how my cheeks are burning. What the hell is wrong with me? Or with Creepy? She wasn't reacting to them like she does when we're around a predator. No, she reacted the way she does when we're around candy.

That only makes her think of *man* candy, and she nearly forces a giggle from my lips.

I grit my teeth, fighting it back. Gods, maybe I need to let her go play with the gators *now*, if only to let off steam. Wrestling with them is her fourth favorite activity, right behind killing bad guys, stalking bad guys, and celebrating both of those things with chocolate banana splits topped by gummy worms.

The thought of ice cream distracts her, but only for a few seconds. I get three steps away from the bar before she's just pelting me with images of slathering that ice cream on those guys and licking it right off them.

Which is *so* not helpful.

Dammit, I need to get out of here.

She doesn't like that, not one tiny bit, and she starts protesting inside of me like a little kid about to go nuclear in a temper tantrum because I didn't give her the toy she craved.

Grinding my teeth, I stride down the sidewalk as quickly as my legs can carry me. Parking tonight was a nightmare, so my car is three blocks away, but at the rate I'm going, I'll be there in only a few minutes flat.

"Hey there, sexy."

Oh, for fuck's sake.

It's not one of the guys from the bar. It's not even anybody I've seen tonight. No, it's just some dumbass in a dirty windbreaker and a Saints baseball cap who thinks my existence means he gets to hit on me.

Lovely.

I veer away from where he's leaning on the wall, avoiding eye contact and sure as hell not saying anything to him while I pick up speed. If he's smart, he'll back off.

If he's stupid, he might be Creepy's second dinner.

"Rude bitch," he mutters at my back.

Creepy snarls in my head. She's sure he's done something we can eat him for.

I tuck my chin and fight to maintain my walking speed. Gods, I shouldn't have come out tonight. I should've just stayed inside, ordered a fucking pizza, and let Creepy pick a movie. She always gets a kick out of the monsters in horror—

Footsteps rush at me. I turn, but someone grabs me.

A biting pressure stings my neck like a bumblebee from hell.

Dizziness sweeps through me hard and fast. I twist to shove the person away, but they move too quickly, tripping me and pushing me at the same time, sending me toppling to one side.

My head clips the edge of a brick wall.

Red and black fireworks explode across my vision.

I'm yanked to the side. Everything is swirling. Pounding. Creepy is just as disoriented, banging around in my skull like a ballistic pinball searching for the way out.

Light glares up ahead. We're in an alley, and the glare is a blazing security lamp at the far end. No one is in sight, and thick metal doors plastered by ripped-up warning signs block access to the buildings on either side. Garbage reeks, making me gag. Or maybe that's the drug.

Because that was a needle that bit my neck, one with a sedative inside it. It's trying to take my legs from me, trying to drag me under the darkness with such force I want to puke from the effort of fighting it.

But here's the thing about Jekylls.

Our Hydes aren't the only ones people should fear.

A dark figure slams my back into the alley wall. "You thought you could kill one of us and we wouldn't track you down, bitch?" Saints Cap Guy glares at me, his arm pinning me to the brick. "You're going to wish you'd left us the fuck alone."

Oh, so he's another trader.

Good.

Twisted words from one of my favorite old tongues spills from my lips, amplifying what I'm about to do. Electricity tangles in my veins, and in my mind, Creepy starts to cackle.

Smoky mist rises around me, glowing as bright as the pink streaks in my hair. It reflects in the widening eyes of the trader and casts a savage neon-bubblegum light on his pockmarked skin.

I've always loved that color.

"*Back off.*" My command sends him stumbling

backward. He trips and falls to the ground. My legs aren't steady, and the drug is still fighting me hard, but while the world spins around me, I brace one hand on the wall and extend the other toward him. "Now *d*—"

A gunshot cracks the air. Pain explodes through my thigh, shattering my concentration and sending me crashing to the ground. My hand grabs my leg on instinct, and blood squelches under my palm as my nerves scream.

Saints Cap Guy shoves away from the ground and stalks toward me, glaring down at where I lie on the filthy concrete. "You're going to pay for that, bitch. Wounded or not, plenty of people will pay top dollar to chop up a Jekyll and Hyde."

Oh, fuck that.

I let Creepy loose.

That didn't go the way I planned.

Admittedly, my *plan* was more like a gobsmacked fantasy that even had Ghastly reeling, and it had only come into being in the three minutes since I caught sight of Mabel, which is not *remotely* the methodical and organized way by which I ordinarily like to do things.

But... dammit.

Keeping my expression politely confused, like any other guy who'd just seen a pretty girl inexplicably pull a runner, I turn a baffled look on Mabel's friend, Tamira. With any luck, the shifter woman won't detect a scent or flinch that might give away the fact my expression in no way reflects how I really feel.

Which is like I want to climb over the table, chase

Mabel down, and wrap myself around her right this instant. I wouldn't even need to let Ghastly out.

My Hyde snarls in protest inside my head, and absently, I send soothing feelings toward him while I try to come up with Plan B. Of course I would actually let him out. Eventually. When Mabel was ready. And when we were sure we could control ourselves.

Because of all of us here, Ghastly and I are the ones who could break her.

The thought makes my Hyde recoil. He'd sooner die than harm her.

But gods, he wants her *now*.

Beside me, a tiny quiver goes through Phineas, but otherwise he doesn't move. It's a testimony to the level of self-control he's perfected, given that Beastly is probably staging a riot underneath his skin. He's been quiet all day, ever since we discovered our quarry had already been killed, and for the first time, I wonder if Mabel is why.

Did *she* take care of the trader? Had Phineas smelled her there too?

I exhale slowly. With the need and longing rioting through me, I have no question she's a Jekyll like us, which means she's also got a Hyde. And if that side of her had been there, if she'd taken care of that bastard, it would explain a lot.

"Um, sorry," Tamira says with a confused look toward where her friend has disappeared. "Not sure what that's about."

I shrug, chuckling and then wincing internally at how strained I sound. I have more control than this. Years of training from my parents, to say nothing of work and school and everything after that, have made my calm, cool mask practically second nature.

I don't want any masks with Mabel.

The woman thankfully doesn't notice anything, too distracted by her friend's disappearance to pay much attention to us any longer. Tamira is a good friend, obviously. Not throwing herself at us or prioritizing gaining our attention over worrying about why Mabel felt the need to run.

But as much as I respect that, I'm also starting to lose it.

I need to go after Mabel. Find her. Learn everything about her and pray to the gods I don't even give a shit about that she'll agree to be ours.

Slithering sensations course beneath my skin. *Our mate,* Ghastly hisses.

My eyes dart to Phineas and Huck. There's never been a question that the three of us would share someone, if we could. I just never suspected we'd find our fulcrum *here*. We'd simply been in town on business, for the gods' sakes, and stopped at Final Toast for a drink because supernatural guidebooks recommended the place. If everything had gone according to my plan, we would've been out of town by sunrise.

No chance of that now.

"I, uh..." Tamira flashes us a distracted smile. "I should probably go see if she's—"

Now I move. I can't help it. No one is going after Mabel but us.

For everyone's sake.

"Oh, that's okay," I say, slipping past Huck quickly and rising from the table. In my haste, I let my limbs bend in ways that would have a human calling 911, but the woman isn't looking in my direction, so she misses the slip. "We needed to head out anyhow."

I take her forearm, my smile never flickering out of place, and let a trace of Ghastly's power run through my fingertips.

She rocks a bit, but my hold on her keeps her from falling. Her brow furrows, confusion in her eyes. Guilt tugs at me for both, but I'm hanging onto Ghastly by my fingernails at this point, and this is by *far* the better option compared to what will happen if my Hyde escapes my control and chases Mabel on his own.

"Go to the bar and get yourself a drink," I say,

letting how much I want her to do that pour through my contact with her skin. "Everything's fine."

To her credit, she doesn't move right away. Her determination to help Mabel is so strong, it makes her falter, shaking her head. "No, I should—"

"Please. It's okay. Just go to the bar."

Gods, I'm begging her, even if only on the inside. But the strength of my need to be the one who goes after Mabel finally wins out. Still looking baffled, Tamira turns away, starting toward the bar like she doesn't understand why she's walking in that direction.

But it's good enough. I take off through the crowd.

"That was fucking dangerous," Phineas growls at me, his long legs catching up to me in a heartbeat.

Behind me, Huck makes a worried sound of agreement. "We don't hurt people. Good people, I mean. She seems like good people."

"She is. And I didn't hurt her. The effect will wear off in a few minutes and she'll be fine. *Confused*, but fine."

Even without looking at him, I can feel the hurt radiating off Huck. "We don't make people do things," he insists.

Fuck, now I feel like scum. There's history in his

voice, and a tinge of disappointment with me besides, and it burns.

Huck has too much experience with being forced to do things. Too much by far. And while yeah, normally he's okay with Ghastly's powers, that's only in the context of using them on *him*, given how they help him with his nightmares and how it feels when we fuck.

In other words, when I have his consent.

"This isn't like that," I tell him. "I swear. Would you rather we were chasing Mabel down with her friend in tow? What if we lose control? Or what if Tamira doesn't even know what Mabel is?"

That shuts them up.

It doesn't feel like a win, though. There's a reason people hate the Ghastlies almost as much as they hated the Bloodies, back before that family line died out.

Silently, I promise myself I'll make it up to the guys —and Tamira—as soon as I can.

We pass the bar, and then the bathrooms, and at every location, Phineas only shakes his head.

She hadn't stayed indoors. She'd been so spooked, she ran all the way to the street.

Fuck.

"Which way?" I ask when we reach the sidewalk.

Phineas casts a glance at the crowd still waiting in line at the door and then puts a few more yards of distance between himself and them, his nose twitching surreptitiously as he sniffs the air. "Left."

He starts off immediately. I jog to keep up.

"When we find her," Huck says. "What will we tell her? Since she ran from us, I mean. She doesn't seem to want to—"

Phineas comes to a sudden stop, every inch of him rigid with alarm.

"What is it?" Huck asks. "What's wrong?"

He doesn't respond. His eyes widen, his nostrils flaring. A tightly restrained growl tries to escape his lips, and then he takes off.

Dread hits me. There's only one thing that would make my friend react like that. "Oh, fuck."

Worry floods Huck's face when he realizes it too. "Traders."

I run.

ICE CREAM
Cookies
CANDY
Candy
Tasty
sing alone
YOU!!

CHAPTER 5
CREEPY MABEL

One heartbeat. Two.

No more hurting people for you.

I flicker fast, disappearing from the sticky ground and reappearing in front of the stupid man with his stupid hat who gave us something that makes the world spin—and not in a fun way. My leg burns and screams, bright blood turning thick and black. It glops down my thigh and calf to pool in my sandal, but I'll deal with that in a minute.

My fist hits his chest, crunching past the ribs and squishing past the muscle, and he gapes like a fish when his red heart comes back with me.

A gasp sounds to my left, and I flicker away before the cracking noises can follow. Bullets hit the brick wall, but the person who fired them can't catch me. I dart to one side, then to the other, flickering in and out of view as I move.

He's just another stupid man in a hat, this time with curly red hair and freckles on his panicked face, but he's going to be dead all the same.

Except the drug is still in me. And my leg still has a bullet hole ruining everything.

I stumble just before I reach him, my bloody sandal slipping on the dirty concrete. The world wobbles and twists, but I still see him aim the gun at my chest, a relieved grin spreading across his face.

"Gotcha, you—"

A dark blur slams into him and propels him into the wall. The shot goes wide, and his scream is cut off sharply by crunchy chewing sounds.

I want to grin, but everything is spinning too much.

Two more shapes appear ahead, blurry and dark against the glow of the streetlamps beyond the alley. One is slender and tall, while the other is funny-shaped. Bendy and wobbly.

But everything is swirling so much that maybe the wobbles are just me.

"Is she okay?" The words are a growl swimming through the soup of my mind, but they come from where the crunching sounds had been. The dark blur can speak, I guess.

That's nice.

"Crunchy-crunchy better not touch me," I threaten, but I giggle too because I'm not sure it matters what I tell him. It's not like I can fight back. I can't even feel my feet, and my hands are thick like clay.

But then, I'm not too worried. The longer they stand there, the more I'm convinced these shadowy things are safe. More than safe, actually. *Fun.*

I giggle again, the world blurring and getting darker around me. I want to get rid of the blur so the shadowy figures and I can be friends. Then we all can have fun.

The bendy one crouches down. Something takes my arms, pulling me upright, but it's squishy in a funny way that doesn't feel like hands. "She's bleeding."

I make a whoopsie noise because I forgot that part. "Sticky, sticky... blood so..."

My mouth stops working and my head lolls because holding it up becomes too hard, and then friendly darkness takes the struggle away.

CHAPTER 6

PHINEAS

She's beautiful, and perfect, and fucking ours.

And those bastards tried to take her.

My jaw aches with the urge to let Beastly return again, not that there's much left to devour of the ones who wanted to steal Mabel and her Hyde away. Between the three of us, we more than dealt with them. And yes, ordinarily we're more circumspect, taking care to avoid leaving any evidence for a crime scene investigator to trace.

But these men dared to touch *her*.

Zeb rolls his neck in a stretch as he walks back to me, every sign of Ghastly gone now. "Fuckers."

I make a sound of agreement, while nearby, Huck hugs his arms to his middle and peers at the green-skinned beauty before us. "Is she going to be okay?"

Heartrending worry fills his tone, the kind that goes beyond mere concern that she hit her head or that she may have an adverse reaction to the sedative they obviously gave her. It's deep-rooted terror I hear, and to another person, that might make him appear weak.

I know differently. Only someone of incredible strength could have survived what Huck endured, and after all he's seen and lost, he has plenty of terrible memories to give him reasons to be afraid.

To say nothing of how *this is her.*

I shudder, too enraged to speak.

"We'll take care of her," Zeb assures him. "Promise."

I nod my agreement, but I can barely take my eyes from the Hyde goddess in front of me. Bending down, I scoop her up from the filthy concrete, careful to support her head and neck just in case she suffered a concussion from anything those bastards tried. If the two men with me were anyone else, I'd be concerned about how they might react to my actions. How I'm silently insisting on being the one who gets to hold her, touch her, and how I'm not letting them close.

But Zeb and Huck understand. Beastly's nature means I cannot allow anyone else to put their scent on her first, even if only in this small way.

I breathe her in as I lift her, and my cock aches, already hard and ready, though I refuse to give into that need with her wounded like this. I first detected her scent when we were hunting that trader last night, a strangely sweet-sour bloody flavor that nearly felled me with its power and stunned Beastly like a bolt straight between the eyes. Every molecule of my being had instantly been aware of what she was to me, and the gods themselves couldn't have stopped me from tracking her.

But when we reached an alleyway, both her scent and the trader's wretched stench vanished entirely, owing to what I now know was her Hyde's ability to disappear at will. We later found the abandoned building where she'd likely killed him, but even then, her scent left no path to wherever she'd gone afterward.

Beastly had nearly shredded the city at that, and I'd been left speechless, too aghast to tell my friends what I knew—that I'd found my mate, and hopefully theirs as well, but that I'd lost her before catching sight of her at all.

Until the bar.

In my arms, she curls up like she was created to fit there perfectly, and her round, pale green cheek rests against me in a way that makes a warm, hungry feeling flood my chest. A tinge of vibrant orange lines her eyes, as radiant and beautiful as a tropical flower. The brilliant hue stains the base of her dark lashes where they rest over her closed eyes, like a sunrise fighting back the night. Her body is delicate. Fragile like a doll, but with viciously sharp nails at the end of each fingertip and a predatory ability that's left me hard as hell.

In every way, she's breathtaking. And though her Hyde is still holding prominence, I can see pink streaks spreading through the roots of her black hair, hinting that Mabel is instinctively trying to disguise the truth of her identity.

Even drugged and unconscious, she protects herself, and pride for her surges within me as I hold her close.

"We're taking her with us," I say to Zeb, brooking no argument. She and her Hyde need to be nearby, if not for all of *our* reasons, then because Beastly is rabid at the thought of not being the one to protect her. But beyond the irrational reasons for bringing her along, plenty of rational ones prevail as well.

The traders might discover wherever it is she lives. A hospital might have spies.

Beastly wants to snarl at either possibility.

Zeb's mouth tightens briefly, his eyes scanning the alley, but he nods. "I'll call security."

There are many reasons I have been friends with this man for the better part of a decade, and his intelligence and practicality are certainly two of them.

While he takes out his cell and begins making calls, I carry her toward the far end of the alley. The bastards hadn't been cautious in their haste to capture her. This alley lies only a short distance from the club, and any number of humans or supernaturals might have spotted them.

But it also leaves us without many options to escape. People loiter all around the club entrance, and security cameras monitor the area as well. Three men carrying away an unconscious woman would automatically cause alarm, and with good reason.

How the hell those traders planned to get her away from here is anyone's guess.

"She'll need water," Huck says, sticking close to my side. "Lots of water. Her mouth will be really dry when she wakes up."

Sympathy rises, but I hide a grimace. He doesn't need to see my pity for how well-acquainted he obviously is with the aftereffects of sedation. "We'll make sure she gets that, friend."

He nods, but he doesn't take his eyes from her.

I glance around carefully when we reach the end of the alleyway. A few people amble across the intersection two dozen yards to my right, but they never glance this way. Otherwise the road is empty, and though the streetlamps create pools of light and deep shadows, Beastly is riding close enough behind my eyes that my vision can compensate easily for the contrast.

Zeb ends his call and pauses at my side, peering up and down the street. "Two minutes."

Irritation makes my teeth clench. "They were that far from here?"

"Party blocking the intersection."

A growl climbs my throat, and it takes effort not to crush the woman in my arms closer to me. It could be a coincidence.

It could also be a trap.

"We need to put more distance between us and this place," Zeb continues as if reading my mind. "The traders could have people coming as well."

I don't bother to voice my agreement, turning instead to the south and striding quickly down the sidewalk, skirting each pool of light from the streetlamps as I go. We're not being nearly as stealthy as I would like, and Beastly hovers close, ready to devour anything that might consider taking advantage of that fact. But Zeb is right. The bastards who hurt her may well have friends on the way.

A screech of tires behind me sends Beastly surging through my muscles and bones, and I barely stop him from taking control. Around the corner, a black SUV makes a tight turn and then heads straight for us, skidding to a halt only a few yards away.

I tense, but traders aren't the ones who shove open the doors and hurry out of the vehicle. Dressed in black with guns at their hips, the security Zeb hired before we came to town rushes toward us, surrounding us immediately.

"Delta team reports a suspicious truck headed this way," the woman in charge announces without preamble.

"Fuck," Zeb mutters.

I don't waste another second. Climbing in with Huck on my heels, I hold Mabel's Hyde close and grit my teeth against the way Beastly wants to shift my bones.

The SUV surges forward, the acceleration pushing me back into the seat. At my side, Huck doesn't take his eyes from the woman in my arms, his hands hovering over her like he wants to touch her but is afraid she'll disappear.

"We'll get her to safety," I tell him.

He nods without ever looking away from her.

The driver curses, his attention on the rearview mirror. I twist to check behind me.

A truck has just rounded the corner. It appears to be a delivery vehicle, though its tall, boxy shape is unmarked by any logos. But around its sides, three motorcycles suddenly race into sight.

They charge straight toward us.

In the row of seats behind me, the team leader mutters something heated under her breath. Pressing her fingers to her earpiece, she says, "Hostiles coming up fast. Bravo Team, you got them?"

With Beastly's help, I pick up the murmur of confirmation from her earpiece, and a moment later, a half dozen motorcycles whip past us on the street, racing straight at the oncoming vehicles. Gunfire breaks out, peppering the walls around us.

"Get down!" the team leader shouts.

I don't need the order, though my size doesn't exactly make it simple. But I tuck down as low as I can, covering the woman in my arms, while Huck does the same.

Our SUV wheels around the corner and speeds off down the next road.

No one follows.

"We're taking green route back," the team leader says behind us. "Everyone copy?"

The pause that follows makes me wince, and when confirmation comes from her earpiece, it isn't the same person as before who speaks.

"Bravo team is down," says the voice. "Delta team copies."

I close my eyes briefly, regret and gratitude tangling in my chest. It doesn't matter that this is what the security team signed up for, nor that Zeb pays them well for the risk they take. I hate that it costs people's lives just to make this world a better place.

The woman relays the information to Zeb and the others in the vehicle, since none of them have the advantage of Beastly's hearing. Silence settles over us, broken only by the sound of the tires on the road.

Minutes tick past. Our destination rolls into view. In my arms, I cradle Mabel's Hyde close, knowing I won't relax fully until she's upstairs and safe, preferably tucked into my bed.

A small gasp escapes her. I straighten, looking down. The green tinge fades from her skin. Her hair shifts fully from black to brilliant pink, the color like joy made manifest, and her nails change until they're painted that same bright shade.

But her eyes start rolling beneath her closed lids. Short, choking sounds leave her throat.

Huck makes a panicked noise. "Oh, no, no, no..."

"What's wrong?" Zeb calls from the front seat.

I have no time to answer as Mabel's body begins to shake uncontrollably in the grip of a seizure.

CHAPTER 7
MABEL

Everything hurts, and for a moment, I want to curse Creepy for whatever the hell she got up to that left me feeling like I was hit by a truck.

Then I remember.

My eyes fly open. The ceiling isn't familiar. The bed or pillows either. The sheets have a rich cinnamon smell that can't quite cover the scent of bleach, and there's no sound of Mardi Gras in the distance. I'm still in my dress from the club beneath the blanket, though my sandals are missing.

What the fuck?

I bolt upright.

Or try to.

Pain lances through my head, and a choked noise

escapes me. I barely make it halfway up before I'm falling back onto the mountain of pillows, my eyes squeezing shut against the throbbing ache radiating from my skull. A duller throb comes from my thigh, and instinct drives me to press a hand to them both as I whisper a spell so softly even I can barely hear my own words.

The pain fades. My breathing slows, the adrenaline fading.

"Impressive."

Oh, shit.

I roll my head to the side, my eyes sweeping everything I can see for the source of the voice but finding nothing. It's vaguely familiar, but that's probably not a good thing.

Traders wouldn't put me in a... what is this? A hotel room? Cages were more their speed. Followed by fighting rings or worse.

I search inside for Creepy. She was the last one of us conscious, and I can't remember jack shit of what went on after she took over.

She stirs briefly. A dull, giggly feeling comes back to me, but it's muffled and dreamlike with no images or explanation to accompany it.

Not helpful. I push for more.

There's a sense of mild irritation this time. Like a

little kid, she swats at me, and a grumbling sensation comes from her, as if I'm being annoying. Ignoring me completely, it feels as if she rolls over, snuggles deeper into the depths of my mind like she's burrowing into a bunch of blankets and pillows, and then she falls back to sleep.

Dammit.

A creaking sound comes from somewhere beyond the end of the bed, like someone rising from a chair. I tense, my mind running through what spells I might be able to use, except I don't even know what I'm facing.

The muscular guy from the table at the bar steps into view.

Shock hits me, but it only lasts a second before rage heats up my veins. He's involved in this?

I knew he was dangerous when I saw him at the bar. But not just him.

Where the hell are his buddies?

"You—" My throat feels like it's full of rocks, and coughing catches me almost immediately.

He circles to the nightstand beside the bed and picks up a glass of water. "Here."

I try to pull away, still coughing, but he just sits on the edge of the mattress and puts an arm around me as if to help me drink it.

I turn my face from the glass. Like hell I'm trusting anything he gives me.

Creepy stirs, wanting to snuggle against him too.

I shove her down. "The fuck... did you do... to me?"

Consternation crosses his face, but then the door opens.

"Is she—" His buddy with the blue-tipped hair stops in the doorway, worry on his face that doesn't go away when he sees me watching him.

"Drink," the big guy holding me orders.

I push away from him instead. My strength is returning. Way too slowly for my liking, but I'll take what I can get.

The consternation on his face deepens, but after a moment's consideration, he lets me go. "You really should drink. Your system reacted poorly to the drugs they gave you, and they made you have a seizure. I was able to stabilize you, but the faster you flush those chemicals from your body, the better."

I stare at him, fear trying to bubble up. Seizure? I had a seizure?

Fucking hell.

Across the room, his blue-haired buddy nods urgently at his friend's words, agreement written all over his face.

Shoving my terror back down, I scoot a bit farther

away on the massive bed, not taking my eyes from them. Phineas. That's the big guy's name. And Blue Hair is Huck. Which leaves—I rack my brain for the name—Zeb.

Who might be calling the rest of his crew of traders, for all I know.

My eyes dart over the room again. I have no idea if the windows would provide an escape, but Huck is blocking the only other exit.

Dammit.

I'm pretty sure it really is a hotel, though, which can't be a good thing. And it basically screams money, which is almost worse. The walls are eggshell white and dotted with paintings that look a cut above the kind you'd find in a standard hotel room. The decor is tasteful and understated, and the bed is massive but not lumpy or clammy. The curtains are edged in gold and pulled tight over the two tall windows on the far side of the room.

Traders aren't poor, no matter how they sometimes dress. They make bank doing what they do because the people they sell to have more money than morals and they're used to using their cash to get whatever the hell they want.

I clear my throat. "Where am I?"

"Our place," Huck says right away.

Phineas gives him a short glance, like maybe he isn't sure the blue-haired guy should have answered, and it makes my skin go cold.

"We were not certain where you lived," Phineas adds like he's trying to mitigate some alarm on my part. "And given... *everything*, it wasn't advisable to risk a hospital."

My heart pounds. "What 'everything'?"

One eyebrow arches like he's Mister Spock. I'm getting the impression that he's scary smart on top of being a killer.

To say nothing of how he looks like he could bench-press my car.

"You saw us, right?" Huck takes a step farther into the room, appearing alarmed and confused in equal measure. "In the alley? Why are you asking what we—"

"How is she?" Zeb's voice comes from behind him, and Huck half turns toward the sound.

The dark-haired guy steps into the room, a tray in his hands. There's a plate of pancakes. A glass of orange juice. Even a little bud vase with a single white flower in it.

What the fuck?

"What is this?" I watch them all warily. "Who are you guys?"

Now they all share a glance like they're weighing who should be the one to speak, and maybe even what they should say.

Rising to his feet, Phineas backs away from the bed while Zeb sets the tray on a dresser and Huck just exhales sharply like he's excited for something. With a short motion, Phineas tugs his t-shirt away and then kicks off his shoes, while Zeb does the same.

My alarm grows. "What are you—"

They shift before my eyes.

Where Phineas stood, there's now a seven-foot-tall creature from a nightmare. His head is shaped like a wolf, but with bone protruding past the black fur near his cheekbones and jaw, like the flesh couldn't contain the skull of the monster beneath. More fur covers his body, but he stands upright like a man, so he's no wolf shifter. He's muscled as hell, from his massive chest to his equally enormous arms and legs, and he has pointed ears atop his head that twitch like they're picking up every sound for a hundred miles. Something green that appears highly poisonous drips from his enormous teeth, while emerald mist rises from his gaping jaw. His hands are massive and end in dark claws longer than my fingers. His feet are longer and covered in fur too, with toes tipped by claws as well. A tail sways behind him, darkly furred but with the end turning white.

Huck is leaner. Almost deathly thin, like an emaciated corpse with his cheeks sunken and his skin drawn tight over every muscle. His arms are too long, like they were stretched on a rack, and his hands hang down by his knees, each finger far longer than it should be. His nails extend like knives growing from his fingertips, and even from here, I can tell they're terrifyingly sharp. He's taller as well, only a few inches shorter than Phineas. He's still got his blue-tipped hair, only now it's solid and spiky like sharp icicles rising from his head. His eyes are huge and shocking electric blue, and they move independently of each other, one rolling to the left and the other to the right and then back again of their own accord.

And Zeb only barely looks human. I mean, he still has a head, shoulders, knees, and toes, but from those shoulders, he doesn't have arms. No, he has tentacles. Huge ones, each coming from his shoulders and stretching to the floor with plenty more rising from his back, all fanning out around him like boneless versions of spider legs. They have suckers on their undersides, each circle dark purple like a bruise, but their other side is deep green like algae. His eyes are white, no iris to be seen, and his dark hair hangs around his face, casting his sharp features in shadow. He looks like an octopus hybrid from hell.

Creepy stirs sleepily in my mind. I swear she purrs with satisfaction. And gods help me, I'm right there with her. I know they should look horrifying. That they *would*, to a human or even another supernatural.

But I'm a Jekyll. They're Hydes.

Gods help me, they are *incredibly* hot.

The three of them shift back. They watch me like they're waiting to see what I'm going to do.

I don't know what to say. I have more questions than there is air in the room to voice them, and the way my body is burning around these guys isn't helping.

Plus, Phineas and Zeb *really* need to put their shirts back on.

But what makes me freeze isn't just the lust currently scorching me or the way Creepy wants to lick each of their bodies like they're candy-coated treats. It's not the way Huck has this eager grin like a puppy who wants me to be excited as well, or how Phineas looks like he's challenging me to shift too, or even how —of them all—there's a guarded tinge to Zeb's expression, like past all his confidence and bravado, I swear he's worried I'm going to run screaming now that I've seen his other form.

Or how it all melts my heart a little.

It's not just any of that. There's something *magnetic* about these guys. A strange draw inside myself that's pulling me to them—mind, body, and soul.

And it's terrifying.

But meanwhile, I'm sitting on this enormous bed in a tight dress, Creepy is stirring stronger in my mind, and my body is tingling at how I'm the fixation of all their stares.

I push away from the mattress and climb from the bed, keeping it between us. My leg throbs like a motherfucker, reminding me I was shot some indeterminate amount of time ago, but my healing spell clearly is working better than I expected because the wound is okay enough that I can stand. "You... How..."

Zeb and Phineas share a glance, and then Zeb gives a short shrug. His confident attitude is coming back into place. Maybe he figures if I haven't run yet, I'm probably not going to. "Phineas and I met at college. We, uh, picked up Huck about a year after we graduated."

My eyes narrow. Picked up? Something about the way he says it makes me think there's more to it than meeting on a dating app or whatever. But while Huck doesn't react to the abbreviated description, he's also drifted closer to Zeb, his body half turned toward the guy, either to protect him or be protected I don't know. But he's barely taken his eyes from me at all.

The two of them are lovers. I'd bet on it. There's a tension in the air between them, and it's not the same as the energy between Phineas and Zeb. Those two, I'd mark as just being friends.

But gods, the way they're each watching me...

Creepy likes it. My body likes it.

My brain is panicking.

Because I want to be thrilled I've met more of my kind. I do. Every lonely moment from my childhood, every minute of feeling like no one in the world could understand what I go through is pressing at me, making me want to feel overjoyed.

But then there's reality.

And the reality is, our Hydes are insane. No one who's met Creepy would think otherwise. And our Jekylls are... well, dammit, *people* with all the complications and messiness that comes with that, same as it does for any other species.

Add those together, and you've got a situation that's at best unpredictable and at worst dangerous as hell.

"And you just... happened to be here?" I manage to make myself say.

Again, that glance between Zeb and Phineas while Huck watches me.

"We were tracking traders," Phineas replies evenly.

"Tracking?"

"It's what we do," Zeb explains in a more friendly tone. "It's how... Well, you probably know. Your Hyde killed the one we were after. We keep our other sides happy by letting them take out the bad guys."

I tremble. That's how I keep Creepy happy too. Hydes have a strong bent toward justice, even if it's their own definition of it, based on their own rules, and doesn't always match what would come within a thousand miles of meeting human legal approval.

"We were going to intervene when the tracker grabbed that woman, but your Hyde got there first."

"You really should sit down," Huck adds. His voice is gentle. Worried too. "Phineas healed the gunshot to your leg, but it'll still take a while to fully recover."

I don't move.

The worry on Huck's face deepens.

"We're not going to hurt you," Zeb assures me. "We, uh..." He chuckles. "We wouldn't dream of it— unless of course you like that sort of thing."

"Do you?" Huck adds, a note of interest tangled up in his anxious tone.

Creepy stirs inside me, intrigued, and I bash her

back so hard and fast, she goes still with shock. I never shove her *that* hard.

Guilt flickers in me, but I can't give in to it. Not when, of the two of us, I have to be the smart one who helps us survive this situation.

She glares at me inside my head. I ignore that too. "Okay, so why are you—"

On the nightstand, my cell phone buzzes. I glance over in time to see Tamira's name flash across the screen.

Creepy stirs in my mind again. She's still irritated at me, but she's also suddenly worried about the call.

I'm just not sure why.

Keeping an eye on the guys, I reach over and pick up my phone. Phineas's eyes narrow, and caution flashes across Zeb's and Huck's faces, but none of them move to stop me.

I lift the phone to my ear. "Yeah?"

"Oh my God, Mabel, are you okay?" Tamira sounds breathless.

"Um, yeah? I..." Fuck, she probably saw me run out of there and hasn't heard from me since. Plus... yeah, I bet my car is sitting on the street where I left it.

Hopefully it's still in one piece.

"Sorry I didn't call," I continue.

"Girl, where *are* you?"

I hesitate, trying to find an answer, but she rushes on before I can speak.

"You've got to get home now, okay?"

"Why? What's wrong?"

She scoffs like it's too much to explain. "Just get here. Now."

CHAPTER 8

MABEL

I barely have time to assure Tamira I'm on my way before Phineas is already heading for the door.

I stare at him. "Wait, where are you going?"

"Something is wrong at your house," he replies like it's obvious.

"How did you hear that?"

He gives me a dry look, and it takes me a second to place why.

And then I just feel like an idiot.

He's... whatever the hell he is in Hyde form, and with ears like that, his hearing must be amazing. So much so that maybe it carries over to his Jekyll form too.

But apparently he's the only one with that advantage. "What's wrong at her house?" Zeb demands.

"Not sure. We need to go."

Zeb heads for the door, but Huck hesitates. "Shouldn't we give her some better clothes now that she's awake?"

I pause, obscurely grateful he pointed that out. I'm panicking a little bit, but that doesn't mean I should just rush over there in this dress, looking like roadkill doing the walk of shame.

Zeb nods. "Right. Yeah." He disappears out the bedroom door, only to reappear a moment later with a bundle of clothes in his hands.

I give him a skeptical look. "You just happened to have clothes here to fit me?"

He grins. "What? We couldn't make sure the beautiful lady asleep in Phin's bed had something else to wear?"

I falter, glancing at Phineas. "That was your bed?"

The enormous Jekyll gives a single nod, but the heat in his gaze belies the controlled motion.

It makes my mouth go dry and my insides twist. I genuinely do *not* know what to say to that—let alone how to feel at the teasing, flirtatious look that's now taken up residence in Zeb's eyes—so I just start to go take the clothes.

My leg doesn't like that plan.

Gasping, I catch myself on the side of the bed as pain rockets through my thigh.

The guys rush toward me immediately.

Before they can get more than a few feet, I've already slapped my palm to the ache and snarled a healing spell under my breath.

They all stop as I straighten. Phineas's eyes narrow with curiosity.

I stalk over and grab the clothes from Zeb. "You have a bathroom or something I can get changed in?" I grit out.

The guy nods his head toward a door I'd assumed was a closet. "In there."

I whirl and hurry toward the bathroom, avoiding all their eyes.

Doesn't mean I can't feel them watching me.

The bathroom is like the bedroom—ornate and vaguely sterile with a feeling of belonging in a hotel. The countertop is marble. The faucet is gold. Little bar soaps sit by the sink. They smell like cinnamon spice, and in spite of myself, the brief thought flits through my head of whether I'd smell these on Phineas if I got close to him, given that this is supposedly his room and all.

"Not helpful, Mabel..." I mutter to myself as I strip

off my dress. Still scowling, I unfold the clothes they gave me.

And pause.

There's a pink skirt. A white tank top and cardigan with little pink skulls stitched into it, so tiny they look like flowers until you get close. The clothes aren't what I expected, but they're also fantastic, and they're going to look pretty damn great with the pink streaks in my hair.

"Maybe they won't fit," I caution myself, not even sure why I care. It's kind of strange, though, to think these guys got me clothing.

And it's just plain uncomfortable in a *not*-so-uncomfortable way to think they wanted to see me in this.

I don the skirt and then get the tank top and cardigan into place before looking at myself in the mirror. "Dammit."

They fit perfectly.

This is too bizarre. I need to get home *now*.

Bundling my dress under my arm, I pull open the bathroom door.

Huck is standing on the other side, an eager grin on his face. "You look amazing!"

There's something so innocent about him I feel bad staying irritated, especially when I'm not entirely sure why I'm upset in the first place. But the idea of hurting his feelings seems a bit like kicking a puppy.

A sexy, blue-haired puppy.

Okay, now I'm just making it weird.

I give him a tight grin as I step past him. Zeb and Phineas are waiting by the door.

"Ready to go?" Phineas asks neutrally. "We had the driver bring the car around."

"The *driver*?" When they don't answer, I make an exasperated noise. "Okay, look, who said anything about you guys coming with me?"

"You expect us to simply wait here for you to get shot again?" Phineas replies.

Creepy rouses with indignation, and I'm right there with her. "You don't get to speak to me like that. I'm hardly helpless."

He takes a step forward and I'm suddenly aware of how much smaller I am than him, even in our Jekyll forms. When he speaks, his voice is a low, possessive rumble that I swear has a hint of his Hyde's growl in it. "And you don't get to die on us."

My body burns at the intensity in his tone, even while Creepy and I both pause at the strange response. It's not just his words. It's the look in his eyes. Like my death would be the worst thing in the world, so awful he won't ever allow it.

Weird doesn't cover this. "I didn't almost die." I hate how thready my voice sounds.

"An inch to the side, and the bullet would have hit your femoral artery. You would have bled out in the alley before we could save you."

In spite of myself, I swallow dryly. I have no idea how to respond to that.

"Is it such a bad thing to have a few allies at your back?" Zeb offers into the tense silence.

My eyes dart to him. I know what the answer should be. Of course not.

Except I've never had anything like that. I've been on my own since Mom and Dad died, and the closest thing I have to allies are the supernaturals who work with me in the underground, rescuing captives of traders and the like.

But my associates in the underground rarely come by, and when they do, they're always on their way someplace else, never sticking around more than a day or so at a time.

It's not the same.

"I need to go." I step around Phineas and reach for the door handle.

"You also need a car," Phineas says, putting his hand over mine.

I pull away. Dammit. "Fine." A new thought occurs

to me. "But if my friend asks, no, we did not spend the night together. Got it?"

Zeb chuckles, and Huck blinks as if in shock.

"If that's what you wish to say," Phineas responds evenly. "So be it."

He opens the door and leaves the room. As they follow him, Zeb grins at me and Huck still looks taken aback by what just happened.

Gods, what have I gotten myself into?

IT TURNS OUT WE'RE NOT IN A HOTEL AFTER ALL. AT LEAST, not any kind I've ever seen.

Beyond the bedroom, there's a kitchen and patio and a view of the skyline that says we're quite a few floors up. The front door opens to a hallway with carpet so thick it could be another mattress, and at the end, there's an elevator that descends with barely even a whisper of sound to hint that it's working at all. The polished brass door reflects us all like a mirror.

Most of us.

My eyes dart to Huck in the reflection. Maybe it's a flaw in the metal, but he doesn't show up the same as the others. There's something blurry about his image. Parts of it even seem to be missing entirely.

The door whisks open before I can ask about it, and the guys move past me, heading into a parking garage that looks like it should belong to a luxury car show.

Lamborghinis. Aston Martins. Things I can't even identify but they look expensive as hell. The guys ignore them all, striding toward a vehicle parked by the exit that looks like a sliver of midnight on wheels. Zeb opens the door with a flourish, motioning for me to climb inside, and Creepy giggles in my mind, pleased by the display.

I keep my face blank while I climb in. I realize Creepy likes them. I have to admit, if I let myself, I could too.

But this is all happening so quickly, and I have no idea what's waiting for me back at the house.

It's hard to relax.

The leather seat wraps around me as comfortably as an easy chair, and any residual ache from my leg or head fades entirely. I stop myself from glancing at Huck as he slides into the other back seat, and I also ignore Phineas when he gets behind the wheel.

"So what's your address?" Zeb asks as he buckles his seat belt.

I tell him. Without a word, Phineas starts the car.

Sunlight filters past the dark smoked windows as

we pull out of the parking garage and onto the road. I glance around, trying to orient myself, and I consider calling Tamira again just in case I can get more information.

But I'm not sure it would help. Whatever's going on, there might not be anything I can do until I actually get there.

Worry tangles in my stomach. My hands knit themselves together, just to give them something to hang onto.

Zeb turns in the seat, smiling that too-damn-confident smile. "So do you work?"

I blink at him. "What?"

"A job."

I struggle to focus for a moment. "Um, yeah. I have a job."

His brow climbs, curiosity written all over him. "What is it?"

I'm lost. "What's yours?"

"This." He twitches his head toward the others.

"I don't understand."

"We hunt things. Bad people. We track them and, well..." He grins.

"It took us a few months to track down the one your Hyde killed," Huck adds. "He'd been busy all over the east coast before coming here. We only arrived in town a few hours before you took care of him."

"I've never been to New Orleans before," Zeb says conversationally. "Gods, am I glad that trader bastard chose this city."

His eyes lock on mine, full of meaning, when he says that. I look away fast.

But then logic kicks in. "Wait, you've never been here? But what about your apartment?"

Zeb makes a dismissive noise. "Oh, that's just some place we rented for our stay."

Holy shit. "Hunting bad guys pays well, I take it?"

"Old family money pays well. Means we can come and go as we please. But we never stay anywhere long. Few days, few weeks tops. Then it's time to chase the next bad guy to wherever they might be hiding."

I can't imagine that. Not the money part or the hunting—well, maybe the money part a bit. But how can they not have any place they call home?

It seems vaguely awful. Like being uprooted forever, living like a dandelion seed with nowhere to land. My house has history. My block and my neighborhood do too. Years and decades and centuries of it, and it always leaves me feeling grounded and stable in a world where *who I am* is only half the story anyone can ever be allowed to see.

And more than that...

Reality sinks over me, turning my stomach to lead. No matter what attraction I feel for these guys, it can't ever grow into anything more. Not when our lives are this wildly different. I never want to leave New Orleans. And soon—maybe *very* soon—they'll do exactly that, and I'll return to being the only Jekyll for who knows how many miles around.

"So what do you do?" Zeb prompts again.

I blink, pulling myself away from the thought. "I... I run a magical apothecary. It's been in my family for four generations."

Phineas glances up at me in the rearview mirror.

"What?" I ask.

He returns his eyes to the road. "Nothing."

Yeah, that's a lie. "*What*?"

Zeb looks between us. "Pretty sure he thinks it's interesting, is all. Phineas's parents ran a shop like that in New York when he was a kid."

He makes the information sound like it's barely noteworthy, but now I'm the one staring at Phineas. Or at least the back of his head, considering he doesn't glance away from the road again.

"So if your family was in New York," I start, "and you all met in college... how many of our kind are out there?"

Silence follows, and my stomach sinks at the awkward tension in it.

"Not many," Zeb says finally. "We've only come across a handful over the years."

"It's part of why we stick together," Huck adds. "So we're not alone and all that."

And gods, if *that* doesn't cut me right to the bone.

Huck's hand twitches toward me like maybe he wants to reach out and take mine, and the ache inside me gets worse. Creepy presses at my skin, reinforcing that pain with the desire to touch him and to tell them all how much she hates being alone too.

But I don't move, and I push her back with a reminder that whatever we say, it won't actually help anything.

We don't want to go. And they don't want to stay.

"We're almost there," Phineas says, breaking the silence.

I look up, craning my neck to see out the front windshield. The turn to my street is ahead, and for a moment, everything looks normal.

Then Phineas steers the car around the corner and my blood goes cold.

Fire trucks block the road. Ash coats the concrete. Crowds of people stand on the sidewalk, gawking, while fire crews pack up their equipment and police try to keep any civilians from coming closer.

To the charred and blackened shell of my home.

"Gods..." Huck murmurs.

It's more than I can say. A strangled cry is trapped in my throat, choking me, and my eyes sting. In my head, Creepy keens with horror.

I tremble, trying to send her comforting thoughts. The structure isn't a total loss. The walls are still mostly standing. Admittedly the bricks and the teal shutters are covered in soot, while the windows are like black pits into nothing, but maybe our home can still be repaired.

Whimpering, Creepy snuggles around the comforting thoughts, hugging them close like teddy bears.

"Pull over," I say to Phineas.

He shakes his head. "We need to go."

"What? No! That's my house."

He slows but only to start turning around.

Screw that. I shove open the door.

"Mabel!" Zeb protests.

Phineas hits the brakes as if in surprise, and I take advantage of the brief pause to get out and race toward the police barricade.

I hear swearing behind me, followed by door slams and hurried footsteps a moment later.

"Mabel! Oh god." Tamira runs up only to slow with shock at the sight of the guys coming up behind me. "Wait, uh... hello." She chuckles breathlessly at me, though the look she gives the guys is more confused than anything. Her eyes linger on Zeb, her brow furrowing. "You..."

"It is *not* what you think," Huck announces immediately, the words sounding far too rehearsed for my liking.

Tamira blinks, obviously hearing that too. "Oh, yeah?" A grin hovers around her lips, though it doesn't quite dispel the confusion on her face.

I can't deal with this right now. "I'll explain later." Maybe. "What happened here?"

"Right." She clears her throat, refocusing. "They don't know. Seems like it might've been a gas leak, but..." She splays her hands like she can't think what else to say.

I head for the barricade.

"Dammit, Mabel," Phineas snarls behind me.

"Officer?" I walk up to one of the cops currently keeping an eye on the barricade. "I need to get in there. That's my house."

The cop skims his eyes across me, Tamira, and the

guys behind me with that look all police officers seem to have. The one that says he's trying to slot us into his grid of guilty, innocent, or a threat.

"Come with me, miss." He nods toward the collection of emergency vehicles nearby.

I start after him, but then Phineas grabs my arm. I look back in alarm. "What—"

Zeb steps up beside me smoothly. He smiles at the police officer, but it's not like any expression I've seen from him before. It's cool. Professional. Radiating a sleek aura of threat and money, like a shark with a trust fund.

"Excuse us, officer." Zeb extends a creamy-white business card he's manifested from the gods know where. I catch a glimpse of an embossed logo that looks like the head of the two-faced god Janus. "Zebedee Chesterton, attorney with Chesterton, Fitzgerald, and Ebers. This young lady is my client. Is she under arrest?"

The cop glances at the card, turning it over briefly as if searching for the trick, and then he fastens his gaze on me again. "You brought your lawyer to a house fire."

It's not quite a question, but I can see the gears clicking and turning in the police officer's head, rearranging that grid to move me squarely into the "suspicious" column with a good chance I'm well on my way to "guilty."

Meanwhile, Tamira is staring at Zeb, Huck, and Phineas like she's not sure what to make of them.

I try for a smile. "I—"

"Don't say anything else, Mabel," Zeb interrupts smoothly. "If she's not under arrest, then we'll be just a moment."

He glances to Phineas and Huck, something unspoken passing between them. Huck takes Tamira's elbow with a smile, and Phineas doesn't let go of my arm while he pulls me back with them. I go along because breaking his hold feels borderline impossible, and because whatever's got these guys on edge, it can't be good.

But I can feel the cop watching us the whole time.

"What the hell?" I hiss at Zeb. "You're a lawyer?"

"Told you I had family money." His normal grin flashes at me for all of a heartbeat, but it disappears fast back into the cold, careful expression he wore only a moment ago. "You see any faces you recognize here?"

I glance around. "I..." I throw a questioning look at Tamira, and she shakes her head. I do the same when I turn back to Zeb. "No. Why?"

"We need to get out of here," Phineas says.

Huck nods fast. He's let go of Tamira, and his

hands are stretching and flexing like his long-fingered Hyde is trying to emerge. With short, sharp movements, he's scanning the street and the rooftops.

"What did you all see?" I demand of them.

"That's not the problem." Zeb is glancing around too. "This is too convenient."

"*Convenient*?" I retort. "How the fuck is it—"

Understanding catches up to me, and dread sinks down into my gut. Oh, hell, he's right. Of course he's right. If I hadn't been so upset about my home, I would've seen it right away.

I nearly get grabbed by a trader who said he was hunting for me, and then a few hours later, my house burns down? And now we're all standing around like a convention of "here be supernaturals" when any number of traders could be getting set to catch us right now.

Gods help me, I'm an idiot.

"You need to get out of town," I say to Tamira. "Right now. Don't go home. Did you bring your car?"

She's staring at me, wide-eyed, but she nods.

"Good. Just drive, okay? And keep an eye out for anyone following you. I'd have you come with us but —" The grim looks on the guys' faces are the only confirmation I need about that being a bad plan. "These bastards are tracking me. If we're lucky, they'll think you're..." I don't want to say human. Not where someone could overhear us. "You know, not worth tracking too."

Her mouth moves for a moment. "Mabel, what's going on?"

"You know that work I do on the side sometimes?"

She nods.

"It's catching up to me."

"But—"

"Please just go. I'll call you in a bit, okay?"

Her face is ashen and she's clearly scared, but she nods again all the same. "Okay." She hesitates again. "Be safe."

I nod. Echoing the motion, she gives a last worried look at the street and my house, and then she hurries to her little yellow coupe, climbs in, and speeds off.

"Miss?" the cop calls from behind me.

"Time to go," Zeb says.

Phineas doesn't wait. Hauling me with him, he strides over to the car while Zeb flashes that rich-shark smile back at the cop. "My office will be in touch."

Ignoring the policeman's protests, the guys bundle me into their car and race away.

CHAPTER 9
MABEL

We drive a circuitous path through town, taking turns seemingly at random, but to my surprise, we end up at the guys' apartment building.

"You sure we want to come back here?" I ask. "What if they're hunting for you too?"

"Two reasons," Zeb says. "One, nobody followed the car, and two, we have enough security on this place to rival my family compound."

"That's a lot," Huck translates for me.

Zeb smiles. "If any traders try to come after you here, they won't make it past the first floor."

I wonder if we should have brought Tamira with us after all. But then, doing that would still put a target on her back.

If there isn't one already.

Phineas pulls into the covered circle drive at the front of the building. "Get her inside. I'll keep watch out here for a bit."

The others nod, and Huck opens the door.

I don't move. Maybe I'm being silly—he looks like a human mountain and he's a Jekyll besides—but I'm suddenly worried for the somber guy. "Are you going to be okay?"

He glances over his shoulder at me, and there's an unexpected trace of softness in his eyes. "I'll be fine. Go."

A quivery, warm feeling tangles in me, but I try to hide it as I nod and climb from the car. Huck motions fast for me to get into the building, while Zeb is already waiting at the door.

The lobby is far from empty when we go inside. Between the elevator and the door, there's a pair of women chatting about something on their phones, a guy leaning against the door to the stairwell texting, and two more working from laptops in the lounge to my right.

As we pass each of them, their eyes flick to us and they give Zeb a brief nod. The women don't even break the flow of their conversation to do it.

"They're all your security?" I ask Zeb while we get in the elevator.

"Plus more watching the cameras and stationed at various points outside."

"Are they… human?"

He shakes his head. "Supernatural mercenaries on loan from Cerberus."

I blink at the name. "The wolf shifters? You know them?"

"*Of* them, yes. Enough to make contact with their people." He gives me a reassuring look. "Trust me when I say the folks who work for them all have *very* vicious opinions about traders. A number of them have lost family to the bastards. We don't have to worry about them selling us out."

"*Especially* with what Cerberus would do to them if they did," Huck adds.

I swallow hard, hoping they're right. I've never met the three wolf shifters known as Cerberus—I've never even met anyone who has—but gods, the stories are extreme enough.

We ride back up to their floor, and I note yet again how Huck doesn't quite reflect the same as Zeb or I do in the mirrored door. Neither of them says a word about it, though, and when we get to the apartment, Zeb unlocks the door, glances around, and then gives a brief nod to Huck. "Stay with her, yeah? I'm going to make some calls."

"I need to do that too," I tell him. At his questioning look, I debate how much to admit, but at this point, I'm not sure my secrecy will help much. "I have some contacts who work against the traders. Rescue their victims. Stuff like that. They depend on me and my home, and they need to know it's not available."

"You work with the underground?" Zeb pauses. "Wait, you run La Fleur, don't you? That's—" A startled scoff leaves him. "That's what your house... Oh, shit."

I wait for him to finish and then nod. "I need to let my associates know what's going on."

"Of course." Zeb motions for me to go.

I can feel him watching me while I take out my phone, and a moment passes before he disappears into the next room to make his own calls.

No one is happy to hear about the fire, and not just because of the traders. La Fleur is a safe haven for any number of groups passing through.

The traders screwed over more than me and Creepy when they burned it.

After I finally get done reaching out to all my contacts, I call Tamira. She's made it safely to Hattiesburg after following a twisting route north, and she assures me she's going to keep going. She's got family in Nashville who embrace Southern hospitality like it's a religion, and they've already got a room ready for her to stay in for as long as she needs.

I think I take my first deep breath in ages at the sheer relief of knowing she made it out of town okay.

When I get done, Zeb is still in the other room on the phone. Huck has stayed nearby, though, hovering by the front door and keeping an eye on the windows like he's concerned the traders will have learned how to fly.

Or maybe he's just watching for drones.

The thought isn't comforting, and I make a beeline for the curtain nearest to me, tugging it closed tighter.

"Well, that's hardly helpful, isn't it?" Zeb snaps sarcastically in the other room. He paces to the door and shuts it, never glancing our way.

I sink down onto the sofa. It's a stiff seat, all satin fabric and wooden armrests. It probably costs more than my car.

Assuming my car is still intact, anyway.

Creepy shifts in my mind, not liking all the levels of uncertainty we're suddenly facing. Her preference is simply to eat or kill anything that bothers her, and right now, we can't do either.

The stiff cushions give a little beneath me as Huck sits down nearby.

Silence reigns.

It grates on me as the seconds pass, like the stillness is turning into needles that poke at me with knowledge of every damn thing that's gone wrong over the past twelve hours.

"So..." I say, unable to stand the quiet any longer. Ordinarily, it wouldn't bother me.

Today is nothing resembling ordinary.

"You all have a lot of contacts." I glance at Huck, waiting to see what he'll say.

"They do."

My curiosity piques. "But not you?"

He turns to me, those icy-blue eyes still so worried, and I swear the concern is for me. "You liked your home, didn't you? It was nice?"

Fuck, this isn't where I wanted the conversation going.

"Yeah." I shrug and hope he'll drop it.

Huck just nods thoughtfully as he turns back to watch the windows and door. "I grew up in a cage."

Okay, not where I saw *that* going either. "Um, you did?"

He nods again. "A wealthy man held me in one. He bought me from some traders when I was small. I don't remember a home before the cage."

"I'm sorry."

Huck shrugs like the past doesn't really matter. "It

wasn't so bad. Not all the time. There were others. Not Hydes or Jekylls. A snow leopard shifter. A pair of sprites. Rare creatures. He had us locked in a secret room, but when he wasn't there, we could talk and tell jokes and things. The snow leopard—" A fond chuckle escapes him. "She was a bit older than most of us. Besides the sprites, anyway. She liked to tell us stories at night to help us go to sleep. Like a family, you know?" He falls silent for a few moments. "Sometimes he'd bring his friends back to see us, though. He liked to make me change into my Hyde for them. Or do… other things."

Nausea rises and Creepy snarls as the pair of us read every possible horrible implication into those two small words.

Huck doesn't look away from the windows. "Zeb says the man treated us all like carnival attractions."

Gods. I search for absolutely *anything* to say after all that, and I come up drier than the Sahara.

Suddenly Zeb's earlier words return to me. He said they "picked up" Huck, like they'd just found him somewhere. It'd seemed an odd way to phrase it at the time. "Were Zeb and Phineas the ones who, um…"

Huck nods. "They got me out."

There's a tight quality to the response, and I think I know the answer before I even ask. "And the others?

Your—" Gods help me. "Your family?"

Huck is quiet for a long time. "When Zeb and Phineas broke in, the rich man started killing them. He was trying to kill all of us so that no one could take us from him. Phineas tried to save more, but... I was the only one he could heal in time."

I've got no words, but in the back of my mind, Creepy is mumbling about her desire for tasty justice, along with how she wants to snuggle our sad Jekyll who almost died.

Shivers radiate through me. He's not *our* Jekyll.

But I still reach over, gingerly placing a hand to his. "I'm so sorry."

Huck freezes. I worry suddenly that I've crossed a line. If he's been through half the things I fear he might have been, touch might not be comfortable for him.

I start to pull back. "Sorry. I—"

His other hand comes to rest on mine, stopping me. For a moment, neither of us moves, like we're frozen on the precipice of something I don't really understand.

"Thank you," he whispers.

Creepy rises up in me like a wave pushing at the flood wall of my control, and in spite of myself, a trace of her green tone tinges my hand while my nails shift until they're partway to being black and sharp like hers.

Huck's breath catches, but a smile tugs at his lips. Icy-white skin lacking any trace of color ghosts around where my hand rests, and his fingers elongate just a bit.

The shivers inside me get stronger. Warmer. Tingly in a way I've never felt. It makes me want to move closer. Maybe to let Creepy come out entirely.

Maybe just to hold him and let him hold me.

Because the tidal wave of this situation is starting to drag me under, and I'm having trouble remembering why it's a bad idea to let that happen.

I force a breath into my lungs, and I pull back. "So you and Zeb..." I tuck my hand into my lap. "You're... together?"

A second passes before Huck gives a small shrug. "He's there when the nightmares wake me. And I... I like touch. And other things. It's nice when it's Zeb. Safe."

Gods, if that rich bastard isn't dead already, I'll find him and gut him without even needing Creepy to show up.

Huck suddenly looks at me, that wary concern back in his eyes. For some reason, though, I swear it's like he's worried I'll draw farther away. "Does your

Hyde have a name?"

I hesitate, thrown by the shift in the conversational direction. "Um, yeah. She's, uh..." Self-consciousness pushes at me. It's a family name, and there's no reason it should be strange to me.

But then, I haven't shared it with anyone of my own kind before.

"Creepy," I admit finally. "Creepy Mabel is... well, *her* name but... my Hyde. You know."

He nods, but he doesn't look like he fully understands.

"What's yours?" I prompt.

"Puck."

I wait, but he doesn't add anything more. "Just Puck? Like... Shakespeare?"

Huck shrugs. "I guess. The rich man called me Huck and called my Hyde Puck. He never said why."

A pained sort of horror sinks over me. Creepy Mabel's full name is a sign of who and what the two of us are to each other. But Huck doesn't know where he comes from. He has no family name. No past. No history rooting him in the world.

Just that secret room and that cage and that bastard I hope is dead.

Aching for all that was taken from him, I want to reach out all over again, but I stop myself. I know what he said about touch, but getting close to Huck—getting close to *any* of them—is just going to be painful when they all go.

"Do you like that?" I ask instead.

He seems confused. "Like...?"

"Your name. And your Hyde's name. Do you two like them?"

His brow furrows. "No one's ever asked us that."

All of a sudden, I kind of want to smack Zeb and Phineas. For gods' sakes, a monster named their friend. A real monster, not just someone supernatural. And those two never thought to ask if Huck or Puck wanted to choose something different?

Before I can figure out what to say, though, Huck nods to himself. "We do. We... Zeb says our names come from troublemakers, and"—a bright grin flashes across Huck's face—"we like that."

My words still fail me, but now it's for a totally new reason. Seeing him grin like that, all playful and devilish...

Gods, he's beautiful.

"We don't want that for you, though," Huck amends, turning to me.

"What?"

"Trouble." He inches his hand toward me again.

I can't help myself. I let him take mine, even if it

just makes the tingling shivers start up all over again. "Why not?"

He looks down, shrugging one shoulder like he's searching for the right words.

"Because you're our fulcrum." Zeb's voice comes from the bedroom doorway, startling me. "Our center to balance us all."

I turn to him, alarmed. "I'm—what?"

His brow rises like he's just waiting for me to agree.

And that's insane. I push away from the sofa, retreating from them both. "You're... I'm not..."

Still sitting on the couch, Huck nods like he's confirming what Zeb said. "You're our mate."

I gape at them, utterly lost for words. It's not that I don't know what they're talking about. Of course I do. Dad always talked about how Mom was the fulcrum for him, and she'd always gotten this secretive, loving smile when he said it. They said they'd been destined for one another, like fated mates among the shifters, but with a quality unique to Jekylls and Hydes.

Because for our kind, finding our mates gives us more than the comfort of not being alone in a world that can't really understand what we are. It stabilizes us, in a way. And at the core of that stabilization is the fulcrum. One member of the mate group who is like the center of a teeter-totter, keeping all sides in balance.

My parents had been rare. Most of our kind were polyamorous and formed bonds with several mates. But Mom and Dad only had each other, and when I was a child, their stories of love at first sight, of just *knowing* they were meant for one another, had always seemed so romantic. Creepy had practically decorated the inside of my skull with little black hearts every time Mom or Dad told us how they met.

But they'd been the two rational adults who'd raised me. Smart, stable people who never did anything more impulsive than ordering a pizza on a Friday night. As I got older, I never really believed they'd simply *known* they were meant for each other from day one. Sure, it was a sweet story, but rational people didn't operate that way. They didn't change their career plans and their living situation and fucking *everything*, all in an instant, just because they met someone.

But this... the way these two are looking at me right now...

Gods help me, it's madness. "You can't seriously believe I'm—" I choke. "For both of you? That... We just *met*, for the gods' sakes. You can't—"

"All three of us," Huck corrects me with a nervous

smile.

"We felt it from the moment we saw you," Zeb says. "Phineas did from the moment he even picked up your scent. Are you saying you don't feel it too? The pull to us? Like magnets in your skin, making you want to draw closer and closer until there's no space between us at all?"

My mouth moves. I can't make a sound.

But he's not wrong, either. My body aches for them. Creepy wants to wrap herself up in them. I've felt a pull to all three of these men since the instant I saw them at the bar, and that hasn't faded, not for a moment since.

Zeb smiles like he sees something of the truth in my face. "We feel it. But you have to choose it too. You know that's how it goes, whether it's one mate or five or three. It's still up to you, Mabel. You and... Creepy, was it? All you and your Hyde have to do is accept us and, well..." He splays his hands like what he's proposing is as easy as can be.

A choked noise escapes me, and my head shakes of its own accord. "I can't... I don't even *know* you. You don't know me. We can't just..."

Uproot my life. Change their lives. None of this works or makes sense, and meanwhile, traders attacked me, my house is a charred ruin several miles away, everything I knew might be ash, and...

And I could lose them too. Like my parents. Like everyone. I could open my heart and end up alone just like I've been for... for...

The room is spinning. Fuck, I can't even breathe. I've got to get out of here.

I race for the door.

CHAPTER 10

MABEL

I make it to the elevator, but before I can push the button, the door slides open.

Phineas gives me one look, and then a tired, irritated expression crosses his solemn face. "We were going to wait to tell you."

I try for a second to get past him, but he's not budging from the elevator. "Why wait, huh?" I snap sarcastically.

"To avoid this."

Zeb comes up behind me. "We're not a danger to you, Mabel."

I choke on a scoff and throw him an incredulous look. "No, you just think a perfect stranger is your—" Gods, we're in the hallway. I shouldn't be shouting this.

I press a hand to my mouth for a heartbeat, fighting to calm down. "It would never work, okay?"

"Are you saying you don't feel anything around us?" Zeb replies, not deterred in the slightest. "You don't want any of us at all?"

My teeth grind. Bastard. He knows the answer. I can read that on his calm, confident face. "I don't even *know you*," I snarl tightly. "But I know it won't work. You all have this life where you never stay in one place for more than five fucking minutes, and I'm... I won't... I don't want to leave my *home*."

My throat closes up on the last words, the fact the home in question just damn near burned to the ground making me want to sob.

Huck speaks up from behind Zeb, his voice sweet and hopeful. "We can figure it out."

I hold back a scoff because, of them all, I don't want to hurt Huck no matter how upset I am. "I'm sorry, but there's nothing to figure out. I'm not leaving town and you are, and I'm not..."

Gods, I don't know how to finish.

Zeb takes a step closer to me. "Mabel, we—"

I try to retreat, but there's nowhere to go because Phineas is still between me and the elevator. "What, huh? You plan to trap me here till I agree?"

They all freeze.

"Of course not," Phineas says. He steps from the elevator and then past me, leaving my exit clear.

I tremble. I should go. Really. Find my car and find a hotel where I can stay by myself and just...

Go.

Creepy makes unhappy noises in the back of my mind.

"You're right," Zeb says quietly.

My eyes snap to him.

He shrugs. "You don't know us. Or vice versa, it's true. And... yeah, there are some logistical realities that..." He trails off as if seeing the anger on my face. "Point is, maybe we are moving fast. Finding you has been... unexpected. But we can't rush you. Or any of this. We know that."

I shift my weight a bit, but I can't make myself get in the damn elevator. Truth is, I don't really want to. I *did*, but only because I was panicking.

But the magnetic pull to them is real, and now...

Zeb steps back, and Huck does the same, leaving the path to the apartment door clear too.

"If you're willing," Zeb continues carefully. "Maybe we could start over? Go slower and get to know each other a bit?"

A quiver radiates through me, made of pain and longing and a need that I know can't ever be truly satisfied. "You're still leaving. I'll still stay. It won't change anything."

"We'd never make you leave your home," Huck promises earnestly.

Zeb and Phineas glance at him. He doesn't take his pale eyes from me.

And after a moment, Phineas nods, and Zeb does too.

"Like Huck said," Zeb agrees, turning back to me. "We can figure it out. But until then, maybe let us try to fix the rest, eh?"

He extends a hand for me to take.

I don't move, eyeing him warily. "What are you suggesting?"

Zeb smiles. "Trust us."

I'M NOT SURE WHAT I EXPECTED, BUT DINNER WAS definitely not at the top of the list.

More fool me.

When we get back to the apartment, Zeb immediately kicks us out of anywhere near the kitchen or dining area. I retreat to the living room, not comfortable with returning to Phineas's bedroom, even if the guy in question isn't in it. Meanwhile, Phineas leaves the apartment briefly only to return a short while later with bags of groceries in his arms. He doesn't say a word as he deposits them in the kitchen and then disappears into what I think is an office.

That leaves me in the living room, sitting on one end of the couch while Huck sits on the other, and for a long while, nothing else happens.

Then I start picking up on smells coming from the kitchen.

Gods, are they good. Michelin-star good, not that I've ever eaten somewhere like that to compare. But my mouth waters and my stomach starts growling almost immediately, the latter reaction reminding me it's been hours since I've eaten and a *whole* lot has happened since then.

At just about the point when my hunger is about to break past all manners and politeness and send me into the kitchen to find out what smells so good, Zeb finally appears at the living room entry. With his cocksure grin well in place, he bows and gestures to the dining room in a flourish. "Dinner is served."

"Shouldn't that be lunch?" Huck points out.

Zeb straightens out of his bow. "You want food or not?"

Huck jumps up to follow me without another word.

Even as hungry as I am, I still stop at the doorway to the dining room, shocked by all he's made in the time I've been sitting on the couch. There's roast chicken surrounded by baked fruits. Potatoes and vegetables all cut decoratively and arranged like a bouquet in a bowl. Bread and salad and soup besides. Drinks glisten in glass goblets, set beside plates trimmed in gold.

Zeb pulls out a chair and gestures for me to take it, that devious grin once again hovering around his lips. The expression doesn't change when I sit down and he pushes the chair in beneath me, nor when he takes his own seat on the other side of the table. Huck quickly drops into a chair at my side, watching me the whole time, while Phineas comes in behind us and sits down carefully next to me, his gaze trained on me like he's just waiting to see what I'll do.

I've never been as self-conscious in my life as I am around these three right now.

"Well," Zeb says with a grin. "Dig in."

The others take up their spoons and forks, dishing out food onto their plates and mine. I open my mouth to remind them that I can serve up my own food, but a brief glance from Phineas stills my protest.

What are they all up to?

Uncertain what to think, I wait until Phineas sets

the plate in front of me, and then I pick up my fork and take a bite of the chicken.

Flavors explode in my mouth. The meat is so tender and moist, I swear I've never tasted anything as good. I swallow it down and look up at Zeb with wide eyes. "That's amazing."

His grin spreads. "Glad you think so."

I devour several more bites before I pause long enough to ask, "Where'd you learn to cook like this?"

He shrugs. "I took a few courses at a culinary school before shifting my focus to law. Or, rather, *agreeing* to shift my focus. It was always my parents' plan. I'd be a lawyer, my brother would be a doctor, and my little sisters will be whatever's left after that. I just... needed to try something else first."

I can hear the complicated tension behind the words, and I opt for the lightest thing I can think to say in response. "Good call."

Zeb chuckles.

Phineas tears off a small piece of bread. "Try this." His voice is quiet, but there's an order in the tone too, and it does strange things to my insides while Creepy coos in the background.

But he doesn't put it on my plate. Instead, he just extends it toward my lips.

I tense, confused, but he only waits there, his brow rising as if silently repeating the order.

The others are watching me, I can tell. It feels like the room itself is holding its breath. But I can't take my eyes from Phineas, and I'm suddenly not sure what would happen if I said no.

But then, it's not like I want to be rude.

Carefully, I lean forward and take the bite from between his fingers.

The bread practically melts in my mouth in a delicious blend of sweetness and spice. My eyes close instinctively, it tastes so damn good.

"Here."

I open my eyes as his thumb traces from the corner of my mouth along my bottom lip, ostensibly cleaning a crumb of bread away.

My insides tremble.

At the center of my lower lip, he pauses and then tugs my lips apart ever so slightly.

My heart pounds. Even that tiny contact has me feeling bound to him, like I could no sooner move away than reverse gravity. On impulse, my tongue flicks out, brushing the pad of his thumb.

A hint of approval ghosts through his expression. "Good girl."

Heat rushes through me, going straight down to my core.

He releases me and I draw in a breath, pulling back, but I'm way too shaky for my own good. Worse, even that small moment has me wet for him.

I wonder if he knows that.

Dropping my gaze to my plate, I try to refocus on the meal. Whatever Phineas is after, this isn't what I'm supposed to be doing right now. This is "getting to know you" time. Not a preamble to fucking time.

Gods, it'd be a really good preamble to fucking time, though.

I clear my throat. "So, um…" I struggle to form words, let alone know what to say with them. "Your family owns an apothecary?"

I keep my eyes locked on my plate as I ask the question, and it takes a small eternity before Phineas replies neutrally. "They did, yes."

Nothing else comes, and I'm not sure how to read his tone—or the fact he just used the past tense when answering me. "Did you like it?"

Another pause, and when he speaks this time, his voice is quiet. "Yes."

My eyes dart up in spite of myself. There's a hint of a pained expression on his face.

Dread sinks over me. Okay, past tense should've been a stronger hint.

Fuck, I think I've stepped in a bad memory of some kind.

He seems to feel my attention, and his dark eyes flick over to meet mine. His pained expression melts away, leaving that same soft, strange look he gave me in the car. One that seems to see right through me, but not in a threatening way.

More like I'm one of those glass balls with an intricate flower sculpture inside, and he thinks I'm incredible.

I can't move. The way he's watching me makes me feel vulnerable and embarrassed and flattered all at the same time. I'm not sure what's going on that prompted such a look from him, but I feel like a fly caught in honey. Dark, deep honey so rich I won't even mind if I drown.

"You're one of the Cormier Creepys, aren't you?" His voice is still so quiet, so thoughtful.

Trepidation stirs in my middle. Where's this going?

I nod.

"We heard of your family, even in New York. You as well. Your reputation in the field of magical healing and esoteric techniques is unrivaled."

My cheeks heat, and in my mind, Creepy preens happily at the compliment.

But then a tinge of his pained look returns, mingled with that softness in a way I can't quite interpret. "What happened to your parents also happened to mine."

Shock makes everything in me suddenly go cold. Old memories, buried memories, flash from deep inside the box where Creepy and I buried them ages ago.

Mom's face so pale and drenched in sweat. The sound of Dad's wet and labored breathing in the night.

How silent the house was… after.

"What happened?" Huck asks into the silence.

I'm baffled for a moment by the question, and then I realize that of course he doesn't know. He grew up in a cage away from any of our kind.

Phineas's eyes go briefly to Huck, but return to mine so fast, I don't have a chance to look away. His brow twitches up in silent question.

I'm trembling and I can't find my voice to save my life, but I manage a tiny shrug because Phineas might as well tell him. It's not like I want to answer the question—now, later, or ever.

"There was an outbreak of disease," Phineas says

to Huck. "Eight years ago. It affected the older genera-tions the worst. A number of Jekylls died."

Gratitude flickers through me for the tight, concise way he describes hell.

Huck's lips part in shock, but he doesn't ask anything else. Instead, he looks at me, such empathy and compassion in his eyes, it's almost more than I can bear.

Phineas's hand takes mine where it rests on the table, and my focus snaps back to him. "You've done well to keep their legacy alive through your work—as well as in the other activities you do at La Fleur."

Something flutters in my chest at the kindness and the way his hand feels on mine. Warm. Stable. Calming somehow. It's such a tiny thing, it almost seems ridiculous the contact should have this much of an impact on me, except I can't actually recall the last time someone took my hand like this. Not to pull me anywhere or shake my hand professionally. Not because I was the one offering my comfort or support.

Just to be with me in the midst of a painful memory.

One that, in our own ways, we both share.

"Thank you." I smile at him. "I hope your parents would feel the same about you."

The kindness in his expression strengthens. "I hope so too."

We sit like that for a moment, and then he takes another piece of bread and extends it to me. "Eat."

It's another order, but somehow, I don't mind. I'm getting the impression this dominant attitude is how he shows his care.

I accept the bread from his fingers, and his smile takes on a dark edge that makes heat rush through me and sends my insides quivering all over again.

"So, um... your tattoo. What's that of?" I turn back to my plate, trying to remember that this dinner is still about getting to know them and *not* about what being near them is doing to me.

No matter how much Phineas appears to be working toward that result anyway.

"A protective sigil," he replies. "One from my family history."

I nod, but as fascinating as that is, I can't bring myself to look at him again for fear of losing control of myself entirely.

Maybe later, though. When I'm calmer. And when I have more than a few feet of distance from that incredibly attractive, dominant Jekyll.

I push onward. "And, uh, Zeb. That law firm you said you worked for. Is that real?"

Silence follows for just long enough that I can't stop my eyes from darting to him. Zeb smiles back at me, but I can tell somehow he isn't unaffected by the previous conversation. There's a serious note to his normally devilish expression. "Yeah. It's the family firm out in Boston, with offices in New York, Chicago, and San Francisco too."

I nod, trying to think what else to bring up that's not them fucking me on the table right now.

"Mabel?" Huck says.

I glance up.

He's holding a bowl of soup with a spoon in one hand and a hopeful look on his face.

My heart melts a little. I lean over carefully to take the spoon in my mouth, and he comes to meet me.

But he moves too fast and a little of the soup spills on my thigh.

I flinch, hissing through my teeth at the hot liquid on my skin, and Huck gasps. "I'm so sorry!" He grabs quickly for a napkin.

"It's okay," I assure him, but he's already crouched down, dabbing frantically at the splattered soup and lifting my leg a bit to get at the drips rolling down my thigh.

Which is when we both realize where he is.

Huck freezes, his expression mortified. He's still

holding my leg. I'm suddenly *so* aware of the fact I'm in a skirt and how close he is to slipping beneath it.

Tingling runs through my skin, same as it did when I held his hand before. It's hot and enticing and though I struggle to find my voice to tell him it's fine, just move away… I can't.

My core throbs. My brain short-circuits.

And my knees inch a tad farther apart.

A tiny breath escapes Huck. His fingers move ever-so-slightly back and forth on my leg, almost as if he's testing to make sure this is happening and that I won't freak out. He's not looking at me, even while I can't take my eyes from him, but I can feel the pressure of the others' stares.

They don't say a word.

Barely seeming to breathe, Huck lets the napkin fall. Slowly, he slides his hand higher, his fingers drifting toward my inner thigh.

My clit aches, pulsing almost painfully in time with my heartbeat out of need for this.

"Is this okay?" he whispers.

I make a breathless sound of agreement.

His fingers roam higher. Brush my panties where they cover me.

I know I'm already wet, but when he feels that too,

a low croon of need leaves him, the sound hungry and not hesitant at all.

My legs move farther apart in a silent plea for more. This isn't what this dinner was supposed to be about, some distant part of my mind reminds me.

Except... this feels like exactly what we should be doing.

His fingers steal past the thin layer of fabric between him and my pussy. For a moment, he just traces his fingers up and down my slit, teasing me and getting wet with my slick. Breathless, I push my hips forward, offering him more access to me.

He dips two fingers into me, and I give a small gasp. They feel longer than they should, but when he looks up at me, I only see Huck in those ice-pale eyes.

"I like touching you," he murmurs.

My breath catches as he crooks his fingers inside me, stroking me from within. "I like it too," I manage to whisper.

He smiles, devious and playful, and it thrills me. His fingers crook again, while his thumb pushes past my panties, finding my clit. "My good Mabel. My belle. Would you let me taste you, my belle?"

Gods, he always seems so nervous that he'll drive me away, but now that he's got me clenching around his fingers, he's focused as hell. Like he's going to use every second of this to bring me pleasure.

And I shouldn't say yes. I *know* I shouldn't. But I slide my hips to the edge of the chair without a word, even if I can't bring myself to look at the other men. "Please?" I breathe.

Huck slides my panties off and then moves my legs farther apart.

"So wet and glistening," he says, his eyes on my pussy. "Do you want the others to see how juicy and shiny you are for us?"

My body tingles with how dirty that feels. How dirty all of this probably is.

But my head twitches in a nod all the same.

Chairs scrape the dining room floor immediately. Zeb comes up behind Huck while Phineas stands behind me.

"Mmm," Zeb hums with his attention on my exposed core. "Perfect."

Phineas's hands slide around my shoulders and down to the buttons of my cardigan. "May we have more?"

At my tiny nod, he begins undoing the buttons, roaming his hands over me while Huck dips his fingers inside me again, tearing my attention between the two of them.

My cardigan falls away. My tank top whips over my head. My bra drops to the floor a moment later.

I'm topless between all three of them and reeling with the fact I'm letting this happen.

But gods, I couldn't stop myself if I tried.

"This is *much* better than dinner," Zeb comments.

I open my mouth to say something in response, but the gods only know what it would have been, because that's when Huck dives between my legs.

Gasping, I buck my hips involuntarily as he twists his tongue around my clit. His fingers start pumping inside me, curling and crooking against my G-spot with every thrust. Phineas's hands take my shoulders, holding me to the chair, while Zeb comes around to my side and flashes me a grin.

"Fuck yes, beautiful," he says. "Let's see you fall apart."

I strain against Phineas's grip, my breath coming in rapid gasps as Huck works me, his tongue curling and stroking my clit until I'm reeling.

Zeb trails his fingers along my cheek. "You want more?"

I don't know what the hell he means, but I nod.

He bends down, taking one of my nipples in his mouth while his fingers pinch the other.

A choked cry leaves me, but Phineas's hands keep

me from lurching forward at the bolt of pleasure that shoots through my veins. He slides his grip up from my shoulders to wrap one hand around my throat, forcing me to lift my head to look at him.

"I want to watch your gorgeous face while you come," he says.

Holy *fuck*.

The other men don't stop, their hands and mouths devouring me like I'm their last meal on this earth. I rock and gasp beneath their combined ministrations while Phineas's grasp keeps my eyes locked on his, his fingers just tight enough around my throat to make the buzz building up in my body even stronger.

I cry out as an orgasm rips through me.

Phineas smiles down at me, all dominant and pleased. "That's our good girl."

I'm shaking with the aftershocks as Zeb moves away and Huck does too, but my eyes are locked on Phineas. The satisfaction in his gaze is mesmerizing. I want to see it shatter as he comes inside me.

I tremble at my own thoughts. None of this is going to work out. It won't and I know it.

But everything in my body is crying out for more, and not just from anyone. From them.

Plates clink beside me. I start to look toward the sound, but Phineas holds me in place.

"Time for dessert," he murmurs.

He releases me just as Zeb suddenly picks me up like I weigh nothing. My skirt falls back into place around my shaking legs, the only covering I still have on. I look around fast to find they've shoved our dinner to the far edges of the table, leaving an empty space near me.

"Will you let us fuck that sweet pussy, beautiful?" Zeb asks. "Do you want to be our dirty, sexy, good girl?"

This is so far beyond what I thought tonight would be like.

"Yes," I whisper.

In a flash, he spins me and bends me over the corner of the table. My breasts and middle press to the wood surface. My hands grip the edge near my shoulders. Cool air brushes my hot core as he flips my skirt up and then moves my legs apart, stroking a hand across my ass with an admiring sound.

I tremble. I'm on display for them, spread out like another dish for them to devour, and dammit, I think I love it. Creepy does too.

Zippers unzip. Fabric rustles, and then a condom wrapper does too. I glance over my shoulder to see Zeb return, every inch of him now deliciously naked with his cock standing at attention for me.

He's stunning. Huge. My needy pussy aches to have him in me this instant.

His hand runs over my ass again. "Such a good girl. So ready for me."

The praise sends a thrill racing through my veins. I spread my legs farther apart for him as he moves in behind me.

He drives himself into me with a single stroke.

A startled cry leaves me, my eyes going wide, and my hands tighten on the table's edge. But the stretch is delicious too, and need pulses through me as my body adjusts to accommodate him.

"We're not done yet," Phineas warns.

I turn my head to the side and see that he's stripped down as well. His cock stands at my eye level, enormous, and I know immediately what he wants.

And what I want to give to him too.

"Are you okay with this?" he asks me, running a hand along my back. My nerves thrill at the possessiveness in the movement, at how he's soothing me and yet pinning me to the wood beneath my chest and midsection.

I nod and open for him as Zeb rocks out of me and then pushes back in. My jaw stretches and I work to relax my throat as I take Phineas in inch by inch.

"That's right," Phineas praises me. "You like me

fucking your mouth, don't you, gorgeous? You like us filling your holes."

My rational brain has totally checked out as I moan my agreement, and he tenses when the sound makes my throat vibrate around his cock. The reaction floods me with the awareness of how powerful I am in this moment. How beautiful and vulnerable this is.

How much I want him to come apart for me.

I press my tongue across the underside of his cock, and he tenses again. I'm giving this to him—to all of them—as much as they're giving it to me, and I love that. It feels right somehow. Like everything is in place, even if that makes no sense at all. I want more than just to fuck them or be fucked by them. I want them in me, with me, filling me up as I make them come undone, and then to never let that go.

Phineas's hand takes the back of my head, his fingers curling in my hair, and a thrill goes through me for the dominance in the gesture, even while I have his cock in my mouth. With a firm grip on my hair, he holds me in place as he begins thrusting.

"You're so amazing like this," Huck murmurs beside me.

My eyes slide to the side to find him watching us, still dressed but with his pants unzipped and his cock in his hand.

That's not enough for me.

I move slightly and reach out to him. Surprise makes him pause, and then he comes closer. I wrap my fingers around his cock and start pumping him too, determined to give him as much pleasure as I can.

"That's right," Phineas says, his voice tight with control. "That's our good girl. But if you want me to pull out, just—"

I shift around and reach up with my other hand to cup his balls, massaging them, and he falls quiet with a gasp.

"You want our cum, beautiful?" Zeb grunts behind me. "You want us to fill you up?"

I want everything.

I moan again, trying to pour my *yes* into the sound. I'm spread out between them all, my breasts rocking against the wood table with every thrust, and I swear I've never felt more powerful.

Zeb's fingers find my clit, and I buck against him. Phineas's motions speed up, his fingers digging into my hair, and the pinpricks of pain only heighten what's happening.

It's sex but it feels like more. Like claiming. Like a shift inside, one I can't turn away from now that it's here.

Zeb begins thrusting harder, hitting me so right it

makes my eyes roll back in my head. "That's it," he urges me. "You take our dicks like a good girl. Our good *dirty* girl, spread out for us because you can't get enough. Just—" A grunt of pleasure escapes him as his fingers tighten on my hips. "Just like that."

Gripping my hair tight, Phineas lets out a choked roar, and hot cum spills down my throat as his orgasm overtakes him.

I'm not far behind. I swallow him down and release him just in time to grab the edge of the table again, clutching it as hard as I can while a tidal wave of pleasure slams into me.

And then I'm boneless. Weightless. I think I cry out but my whole body is lost to a rush of white-hot light, everything drowning in sheer, blinding pleasure.

Holy shit, I've never come this hard in my life.

Shuddering all over, I return to earth just in time to feel ropes of Huck's cum splatter my skin, while behind me, Zeb thrusts into me hard and fast with a cry of his own.

Panting, I lie there between them all. My arm and side are sticky with Huck's release, and a moment later, he reaches over, smearing his cum even farther across my skin.

"Mine," he growls, and I hear his Hyde in his voice. "Ours."

A flutter of arousal pulses through me all over again at his possessive action. I feel every inch their dirty girl, and I think I'm in heaven over it. I never imagined anything like this, but right now, it's all I want.

Even if it won't work out.

I hate the thought. Hate that it's trying to steal this moment, and Creepy bats the whole idea away from her corner of my mind. But the ecstasy of this is now cracked and damaged, and I can't stop how my contentment fades when Phineas pulls me upright from the table.

Tonight was amazing, yes. I've never come like that, not ever. But I can't give up my life for sex. For orgasms. I can't walk away from everything just because these men fit something inside me I never knew needed fitting.

"Let's get you cleaned up," Phineas says, leading me toward the hall.

I nod and go with him, but it's a struggle not to feel like I'm lying when I smile. I want these men. Want more of what we shared.

But even though everything's shifted, nothing's changed.

And in the end, it's still going to fall apart.

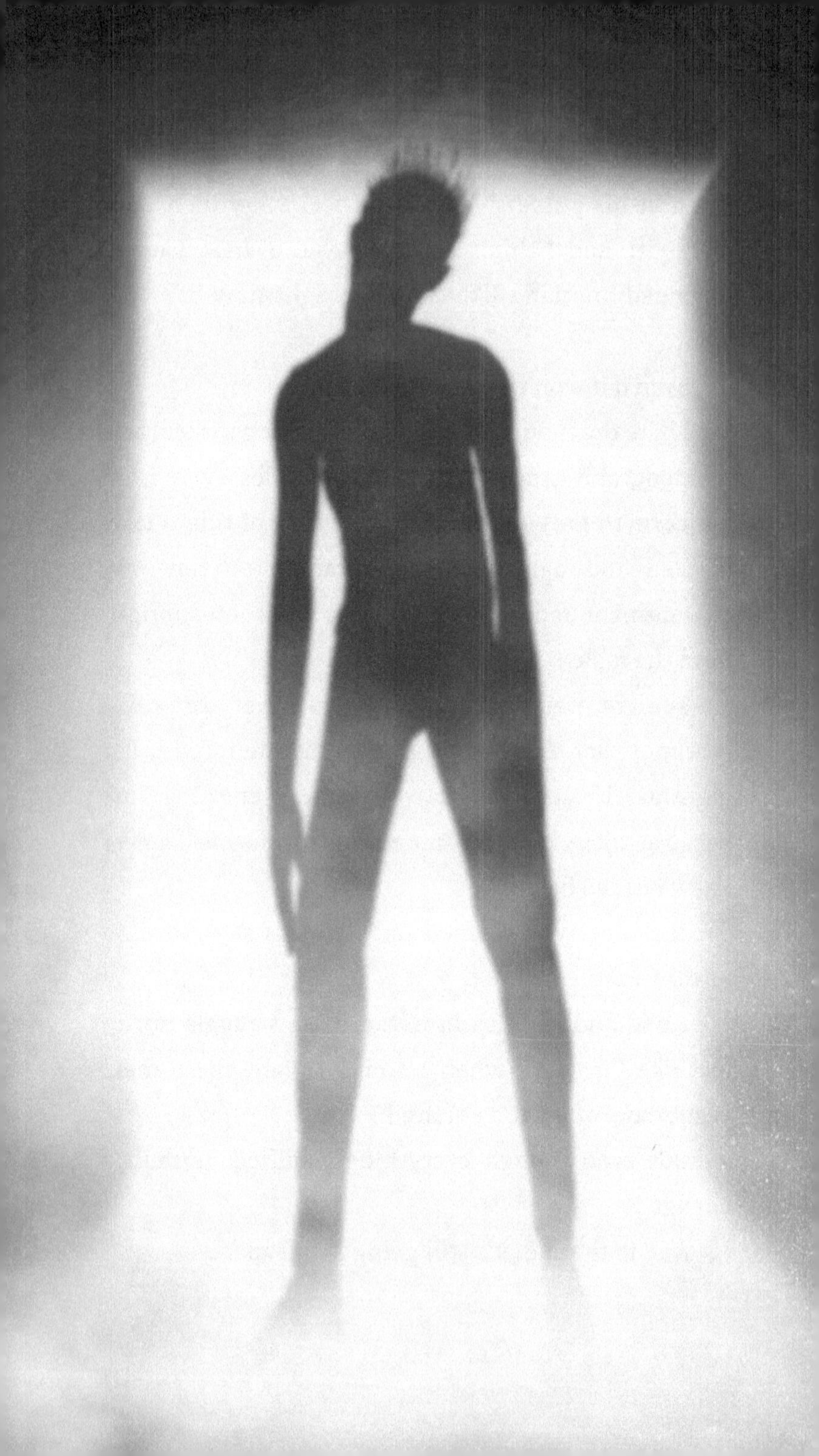

HUCK

Mabel's taste lingers on my tongue. My eyes track every inch of her nakedness while she follows Phineas down the hall, and my body hums with the urge to do more than cover her with my cum. I need to fill her. Claim her. Keep her with us always.

Except... I'm not sure I can.

Trailing Mabel and my friends to the main bathroom, I chew on my lip, at a loss for what to do. It's my fault, really. I started this, touching her, tasting her like that. The way I feel around her is like gravity, inescapable, and my need for her is as well. As long as I could control what I did while around her, it was okay. But I should've known better.

I should've known what that would lead to.

My heart pounds, and my skin burns, every nerve on fire with remembered pain, taunting me. On autopilot, my mind repeats the soothing mantras the sprites taught me when I was little and the rich man would come.

But the rich man is the point. He's the problem.

So the mantras don't help much at all.

Phineas opens the door, and the smell of lavender and spice joins the scent of Mabel's arousal on the air. Puck wants to drink it in. To make her come and come until she passes out from the pleasure.

But we can't. He knows it. There's a reason we didn't get naked with the others at dinner.

There's a reason we probably never will.

I stop in the hallway, watching through the door as Phineas turns on the hot water and then brings Mabel to him. The spray rushes over her and sends clouds of steam rising from the shower floor. She doesn't pay attention to any of it, instead focusing on sliding her hands up Phineas's dark chest like she loves every inch of what she's touching.

Puck buries himself deep in my mind, hiding from the pain of how no one will ever touch us like that by wrapping himself in the safe, cozy darkness. And I look away. I want to retreat too, except I'm the one in charge of our body right now, and moving might draw her attention.

"Hey." Zeb's voice is soft.

I glance up. He's at the doorway, and he slips out of the bathroom while Phineas starts kissing Mabel.

My lip hurts. I'm chewing on it too hard.

"You don't have to do this," Zeb murmurs, drawing me away from the door.

Anguish gnaws at me as I nod. Zeb understands. I know he does.

It just doesn't make the truth hurt any less.

"But..." he continues, glancing back at the bathroom briefly. "If she's going to be ours, we need to give her the chance to love *all* of us, right?"

My eyes dart away, skipping around the hall like Puck has control of them.

Zeb's familiar touch on my cheek draws me back around. "Trust that pull inside yourself. The one that says she's our mate."

I nod because I know he wants me to, but that doesn't mean I can believe him. Or, really, believe myself. I want her. I know that. But I want good things for her too, and that...

Maybe that's not me.

A breath leaves Zeb like he sees where my thoughts have gone anyway, and pain stirs in me for him. I'm being selfish, keeping the focus on myself. He's got his own reasons to be nervous about being with her.

I mean, yeah, I'd been mad at him for how he used Ghastly's powers on that girl at the bar. But I'd been mad because that *isn't* him. He doesn't manipulate people, even though he could. He doesn't hurt people, even though the gods know he has the power to wreak havoc.

He's scared he'll hurt Mabel.

I know he never would.

"You too," I say. "You... you trust that pull too. And trust *you*." I squeeze his hand. "I do."

He chuckles softly, gratitude in his eyes.

"Are you two coming?" Phineas calls. "Or do I get our sexy girl all to myself?"

Zeb grins at me. "Come on." He kisses me, a teasing brush of his lips, and he gives me that focused, confident look he does so well. The one that says he believes in me. The one that says I'm not broken at all.

I smile like it's working, just enough that he goes on ahead, and it isn't until he disappears into the bathroom that I let the expression crack into pain. But then hungry sounds come from beyond the door, and kissing too, and Mabel giggles at whatever he's doing.

It makes my heart ache.

But it pulls me back to the doorway all the same.

It's just like gravity.

The erotic scene before me is beautiful, like a picture. Mabel's legs are wrapped around Phineas, and he's gripping her ass while he drives into her. Zeb is behind her, his cock buried in her rear entrance. One of his hands has her breast, pinching and rolling her nipple, while his other has stolen around her front to massage her clit. Her head is thrown back, her pink-streaked hair falling over Zeb's shoulder, and her eyes closed, ecstasy painted across her face. Gasping pleas escape her, begging them for more, more, just like that.

Before I even realize I've moved, I'm gripping my cock, stroking it hard. It's that or rush over there, and gods forbid she wants me to join in.

But maybe she'll be too sated. Maybe they'll exhaust her. Maybe—

Her cries when she comes steal my breath. I drink in the sight of her release while Zeb and Phineas grunt and thrust harder, overcome by their own pleasure.

Gods, if she could make those sounds for me. If I could just...

Mabel's eyes find mine. Sweat clings to her skin, making it glisten. Her lips are parted, her chest rising and falling fast from the exertion. She smiles breathlessly and reaches out a hand to me.

I freeze. I've fucked up. I shouldn't have—

Her brow furrows. "Huck, are you okay?"

I scramble for words. "Y-you're tired. You should rest."

It's a plea more than anything, and she seems to hear that.

Her eyes narrow. Carefully, she eases away from Zeb and Phineas, and panic grips me when she comes closer, deliciously naked and freshly fucked yet still looking ready for me.

I retreat.

She stops. "What is it?" At my silence, uncertainty flashes over her face, and she pulls a towel from the rack, wrapping it around herself without ever really taking her concerned gaze from me. "Is something wrong?"

I'm ruining everything. I know that. I'm watching everything tumble downhill like an avalanche and it's all my fault.

Past Mabel's bare shoulder, Zeb and Phineas are watching me. Zeb's brow rises, silently urging me to speak, but I can't. I don't want to see her pull away. To watch her recoil and then try to hide the reaction.

Because she would. She's nice. Kind too. I've only known her a short while, and already I've learned that much about her.

She'd try not to hurt my feelings.

But that wouldn't change the truth.

"We don't have to do anything," she offers, tucking the towel up higher around her gorgeous breasts. "Not if you don't want to."

My head shakes. I can't help it. She's protecting herself from me in that gesture, and it makes my insides twist like there's a knife in my stomach. "It... it's not that."

She hesitates. "Okay."

The silence grows.

"Tell her, Huck," Zeb murmurs gently. "Trust, remember?"

My eyes squeeze shut. "I just... I don't want you to... to be disgusted by me."

More silence follows, and it's awful. I force myself to open my eyes.

She's staring at me, utterly baffled. "Why would I ever be disgusted by you?"

I find Zeb and Phineas again. They don't speak this time.

They're leaving it up to me, what I say. How much I tell her.

I swallow hard. Brace myself. And I yank my shirt over my head.

I can hear the moment she sees it all. The way her

breath hitches in a tiny gasp. The small exhalation of shock that follows.

Maybe the floor could open up and swallow me. Maybe the power could go out, letting darkness take us long enough for me to run.

Neither happens, but that doesn't stop shame from rising like a tidal wave eager to make me drown. I scramble to pull my shirt back on. "I-I'll go. I'm sorry. I—"

Her hand catches my arm. I freeze all over again, my eyes darting to hers on instinct.

The fierceness in her gaze stops my world.

"Did..." Her voice is a growl, and she shudders like she's holding her Hyde back. "Did *he* do this?"

My head twitches in a tiny nod.

Her hand shakes, her fingers tightening on my arm. But a pained look starts to creep into her eyes as the seconds tick by. "Did you think I wouldn't want to be with you because of it?"

Shame grows. I can't hold her gaze.

I shrug.

She's silent for a moment. "May I touch you?"

My eyes snap to her in shock. "You... you want to...?"

"Only if it's okay with you."

I manage to twitch my head again, and I can't breathe while her hand comes toward me.

But she's going to change her mind. I know it. She has to. At any moment, she's going to—

Shivers course through my body when her palm gently rests on my abdomen. I watch as her fingers trace across my skin, mapping the pits, the valleys. The old burns and the twisted scars. Slowly, she walks around me, her hands ghosting across the puckered bullet wounds on my shoulder. The acid and cigarette burns on my ribs. The places where he carved into me, just because he could.

Her breath catches at the slashes that crisscross my back. "He whipped you too?" she whispers.

"H-his friends, mostly. Before... other things."

Air rushes from her, but her fingers stay on me, drifting along until she pauses directly behind my back.

I tremble, wondering if it's too much. If she's been suppressing her revulsion until she was beyond my line of sight, and now she—

Her lips touch the place where my neck meets my shoulders. The marks are bad there. I've seen them in the mirror. He tried to hang me that day.

I can't breathe now either.

"Is he dead?" she asks. "Are all of them?"

I nod and try to find my voice. "After Phineas healed me, we tracked them. We found his friends near Boston. Found him three months later outside Cincinnati. He... he was trying to start another collection." A shiver runs through my body. "I made sure none of them could hurt anyone ever again."

Mabel circles me, her hand lingering on my skin until she's in front of me once more. Her eyes meet mine. "Good."

She says it with such unwavering conviction, nothing in her voice could give me room for any doubt. There's a bloodthirsty light in her eyes too, a gleam from her Hyde that says if I hadn't killed them, Creepy would have hunted each of them down, because there's no question in her mind that they needed to die.

Something inside me quivers.

Mabel steps closer. That bloodthirsty light fades, turning to a quiet insistence that rivets me in place. "None of this changes how attracted I am to you, Huck. Not one single bit. And I swear to you on my *life*, I'm not disgusted by you."

I can't look away from her. In my chest, something breaks, painful and yet warm. It spreads like fire through my veins, pulling on me like gravity, urging me to fall.

And I let go.

I rip my pants away, ignoring how the fabric tears. I grab her, driving her back toward the shower while Phineas and Zeb clear out of my path. Mabel gasps, but there's no fear in the sound. Water splashes us, but I couldn't care less. Distantly, I feel Zeb shove a condom into my hand, and I roll it on purely by autopilot, scarcely letting my lips leave hers long enough to breathe.

Because I just want to keep kissing her. Touching her. I lift her up, pressing her back into the tile wall as her legs wrap my hips, and then...

A groan escapes me as I sink into her pussy. She's perfect. Everything I never knew I needed and more. I rock my hips forward over and over, drowning in the feel of her, claiming her with everything I have.

Because she's mine. Ours. Puck surges up to ride just beneath my skin, relishing the scent and taste and feel of her, eager for when he can claim her too.

"My belle," I gasp with every thrust. "My belle."

Once upon a time, the snow leopard shifter told me *belle* meant beauty, and that there'd been a woman with that name who loved a monster no matter what he looked like.

I never dreamed that story could really be true for me.

Gasping with pleasure, I clutch Mabel to me as she comes on my cock, her pussy fluttering like she wants everything I have to give. There's no one in this world who'll ever be as beautiful to me as her. No one I'll ever love more. She's my belle. My everything.

And whatever happens, I'll be hers until the end of time.

CHAPTER 12
MABEL

I'm damn near limp in Huck's arms after he gets through with me, reeling from the fact I've lost count of the orgasms these men have wrung from my body.

And from what I learned about Huck.

I've always prided myself on how I try to seek justice through legal channels if I can. How I'm not like Creepy in that way. But when I saw the hellscape of scars on that sweet Jekyll's body, the layers of countless marks that could only be burns and bullet wounds and—gods—whips too, every thought of *legal* justice went out the window.

I'd wanted blood for what Huck and his Hyde had been forced to endure, and my relief at finding out those bastards are dead was so intense, it left me shaking.

I wrap my arms around the sweet Jekyll as he carries me out into the hall. After he finished making me come against practically every wall and counter in the bathroom, Huck insisted on being the one to clean me up, shampooing my hair and washing me down from head to toe.

It'd been so hot, I ended up fucking him again in the shower afterward.

Phineas and Zeb follow as Huck carries me. I'd already respected these men, but seeing how those two supported their friend brought that respect to a whole new level. They both obviously knew what it meant for him to show me his body like that, and how hard it must have been for him to work past the fear I'd reject him over it. And even once he took that leap, they hadn't taken it for granted or treated it like they'd gotten something out of the way. No, they let him have the lead in our sex-capades, never once pushing him aside, and all without a single trace of jealousy, impatience, or irritation.

They're good men, all of them. My heart hurts for how clearly I can see that and for how it makes me wish things between us really could work out.

But it can't. I know it can't. It'd be the most selfish

thing on earth to ask them to give up rescuing supernaturals. For pity's sake, Phineas and Zeb doing what they do is *probably* why Huck is even here right now, instead of trapped in hell or dead in a cage. He's living proof they have to move on soon, for the sake of everyone who needs them out there.

And I can't leave my home. Even if traders were the ones to burn it, there's a chance the ones in the alleyway had been the arsonists, and now they're gone. Traders are notoriously insular, after all. Crews never share secrets, whether it's tactics for catching supernaturals or places where they might be found. This is a business to them. Competition is fierce.

So if those assholes in the alley were the extent of these traders' crew, no one else might know La Fleur's location, which means going home could be safe after all. And people in the underground depend on La Fleur. They depend on *me*. Phineas wasn't wrong about the magic I do. The help I give people who come through my door. I can't walk away from that.

It's just that somewhere in the past few hours, I screwed up. I lost my nerve. I got too close.

And now the fact they have to go hurts like absolute hell.

Huck snuggles me closer when we reach the living room, murmuring the sweet nickname he gave me and placing a kiss on my temple before setting me on my feet again. I do my best to shove the pain down, focusing on this moment instead of everything that's going to come after. Even if it's going to hurt when they go, for right now, they're here and that's what matters.

At least in the future, I'll be able to look back and know I enjoyed the memory when it was real.

My legs feel like wobbly noodles beneath me, but Huck doesn't let me go, supporting me while Zeb disappears down the hall for a moment and then returns with clothes bundled in his arms.

"So," Zeb says as I pull on sweatpants and a black t-shirt that's so big, it must belong to Phineas. "How about a snack, hmm? Since dinner was interrupted."

I eye him. "Like a *food* snack or...?"

He grins, but there's an amused cast to his expression. "Food. You need to eat." He shrugs. "We probably do too."

He twitches his chin toward the couch and then heads for the kitchen. Dressed in gray sweatpants and a t-shirt of his own, Phineas takes a seat near me and grunts something that sounds like "scoot." Before I can ask what he means, he takes my legs and pulls them around, placing my feet on his lap.

And then he starts rubbing them.

Oh gods, that's good.

Huck climbs onto the couch beside me and then clambers around so that his knees are on either side of my hips. I look behind me, confused, when suddenly he starts massaging my shoulders.

Wow, these guys are laying it on thick.

But you know what? I'm damn well going to let myself enjoy it.

If only for tonight.

Closing my eyes with all the resolve I can muster, I sigh and lean back into Huck.

He murmurs happily, nuzzling the side of my head in a motion more like a wild animal than anything. "Maybe we could watch a movie? Do you like movies?"

I nod.

"What kind?" he asks.

I hesitate because I'm not sure how they'll take the fact Creepy and I enjoy horror as long as it's not nihilistic. But I guess hiding what I enjoy isn't good for anyone, least of all me.

When I tell them, Huck beams and even Phineas smiles. "Oh, we love a good horror movie!" Huck cries. "Zeb! She likes horror movies!"

Zeb comes back in with a tray of fruits, cheeses, and crackers. "So what're we watching?"

"What about that new one with the family in the haunted house?" Huck suggests.

At the guys' questioning glances, I nod. "Sounds good to me."

Putting the tray down on the coffee table, Zeb settles in on the floor in front of me.

"You sure you're comfortable?" I ask him.

He nods and picks up a cherry, turning a bit to offer it to me. "Definitely."

I don't think I've had this much fun watching a movie in years. It's not just the food or how relaxed the guys have made me feel. Even though I technically just met them a short time ago, there's something so comfortable about being around them, like I've known them for years. Before the movie is over, I end up dozing off with Huck's arms around me and my feet beneath a blanket on Phineas' lap, feeling more comfortable than I think I've ever been, even in my own bed.

A muffled cry pulls me from my sleep.

I look around, confused. I'm still on the couch, though now my head is on a pillow and the blanket is tucked around me. The living room is mostly dark, but enough ambient light from the city slips past a crack between the curtains to thin the shadows. Phineas rests in an armchair nearby, his hands folded over his middle and his legs crossed at the ankles. His chest rises and falls in a steady rhythm. Huck lies on the blankets spread on the floor, his back to me, while Zeb is in another chair nearby.

In the darkness, Zeb is watching me.

I push away from the couch. "Was that you?" I whisper.

His head shakes, but he doesn't appear concerned. More like he's resigned.

Wariness prickles through me. Why does he look like that? That cry sounded so scared. Why wouldn't he want to know where it came—

Huck suddenly twitches beneath his blanket, whimpering.

Zeb sighs and gets up.

I do the same, my apprehension replaced by concern. "What's going on? Is he—"

Zeb holds up a hand. "It's okay. Just a nightmare. Go back to sleep." He walks carefully toward Huck, who's started shaking under his blanket.

I stare after him for a heartbeat and then cast a quick glance toward Phineas. The other man's eyes are open now, but he's making no move to follow. Instead, when he sees me look at him, he just nods briefly at the couch as if silently repeating what Zeb said.

Which is ridiculous. I'm supposed to just roll over

and ignore this, especially after everything I learned about Huck today?

A grim sense of *hell no* comes from Creepy.

I start after Zeb.

"Mabel," he whispers when he realizes I'm following. "It's okay. Huck just has bad dreams sometimes."

"From what he went through," I fill in.

Zeb pauses. "Yeah." He glances down as a murmured plea for someone to stop comes from Huck. "It's hard to wake him most of the time. Even..." He grimaces briefly. "Even for me. But if they wake up and the two of them don't realize they've been dreaming, Puck can get violent. It's best to just let them find their own way out."

Creepy doesn't like that either. She shivers through my skin, wanting to cuddle our Jekyll close and somehow fix it all.

I exhale slowly, reminding her he's *still* not our Jekyll. He can't be, not for real.

She doesn't care. Not when he's in pain and we're not helping him. We can handle violence. So there's no excuse to leave him suffering.

And to be fair, she has a point there.

I step past Zeb, ignoring his stifled noise of protest as I crouch down beside Huck. Beneath his tousled white and blue hair, his pale face is screwed up tight like he's cringing away from something. Every few seconds, he flinches like he's being shocked.

Which, based on his scars, he probably was back then.

Creepy won't stand for it, but I barely need her encouragement to pull the edge of the blanket aside and slip in next to Huck. He's shirtless beneath the blankets, wearing only a pair of sweatpants to cover his lower half, and it makes something inside me ache to know he'd finally been comfortable enough around me to go uncovered like that. But when I gently put my arm over his side, I can feel the cold sweat covering his scarred skin. "Shh," I whisper. "You're safe. We're here."

He twitches harder, mumbling things I can't understand.

"Mabel..." Zeb sounds worried.

I chew my lip. Surely, Phineas and Zeb have already tried various techniques to help Huck and Puck. I can't imagine there's anything I can do that the two men haven't already thought of.

Creepy pushes at me again, refusing to accept that answer.

Okay then...

I close my eyes, focusing on Huck's tense body

beneath my arm. The soothing spell my mother used when I was a child spills effortlessly from my lips.

Huck whimpers briefly and then suddenly switches to an angry mumble, a sibilant quality to the sound that makes me suspect Puck is trying to emerge.

I focus harder, murmuring the spell over and over until the words and sounds loop so seamlessly, even I can barely track where they begin and end.

Prickles course through my skin. My nails tingle as they lengthen. I don't need to see them to know they're turning black.

Creepy's not waiting. She wants to help, and I can't begin to predict what she'll do if Puck attacks us.

Or what Puck will do if he sees her as a threat.

I squeeze my eyes shut more tightly, trying to focus on staying here and not letting the shift take me.

The shivers on my skin get worse. Whispering sounds flit around me, there and gone like they've been whisked away by a breeze, and I have no idea where they're coming from. My throat aches as Creepy suddenly tries to interrupt the spell, and I cling to my own words as I resist her.

With every passing second, the whispers get louder.

Is this Puck? Is he doing something to fight me and she's reacting to it?

A tingling sensation passes over my skin like a cold breeze licking at me. My eyes open.

Ghostly pockets of mist twist in the air above us. They stretch toward Huck, and every time a tendril touches him, he flinches.

Holy shit.

Creepy's voice breaks past my own. *"Not for you. Stop what you do."*

A cold sensation rushes over me, prickling like an icy river. The mists retreat, pulling away from Huck, and then they scatter like they've been swept away by a strong wind.

I tense. Creepy did that. Moreover, I think I know what just happened. Creepy and I share memories from time to time, but the ones from her are often strange and fragmented. They don't always make sense.

But I know what she can see, which means I know what those things really were.

The dead. Lost souls drawn to him because of either his pain or his guilt at being the only one of his family to survive.

Except... Creepy spoke to them and they reacted, and I have enough of her memories to know *that*, at least, is not normal.

As the mists vanish, Huck stills. His rapid

breathing slows, and the tension leaks from his body. I let out a breath in relief that somehow, we've given him a reprieve. Everything else can be figured out later.

But the peace only lasts for a moment.

Before I can even gasp, Huck shifts, and suddenly Puck is there. His long legs wrap mine in a jiu-jitsu-style move, and the blanket falls away as he rolls me quickly until he's lying on top of me. Lightning fast, my arms are pinned above my head and my body is immobilized under him while one of his long-fingered hands wraps around my neck.

Oh, shit.

CHAPTER 13

MABEL

"Puck, don't!" Zeb reaches for us.

The Hyde snarls like a wild animal, his jagged teeth glinting like metal in the shadows. His free hand lashes out, his too-long fingers curled and his nails looking every bit like knives. The threat is clear, and Zeb slams to a halt at it.

One of Puck's wide, electric-blue eyes watches the Jekyll while the other stays locked on my face, but when Zeb doesn't come closer, both roll back into place to stare down at me.

I don't move.

A low growl rumbles from Puck. He's scarred like Huck, his torso practically forming a topographical map of hell, but nothing of Huck's sweetness is in his eyes. His mad gaze is pure predator, deranged and totally feral. His lips pull away from his metal teeth, his mouth gaping like a too-large and distorted rictus from a skull, ready to bite me. Slowly, his fingers tighten on my neck, his knife-like nails pricking my skin until they're at the edge of drawing blood.

"Not... your enemy," I gasp, fighting to keep Creepy from taking over and turning this into a brawl.

The growling gets stronger. Hungrier. From the corners of my eyes, I can see Zeb and Phineas standing on either side of us, clearly torn between yanking him away and the possibility that they'll make this worse.

But then Puck draws in a deep breath like he's sniffing me. The growling changes, still hungry but now with approval in the sound. His crazed eyes never leaving me, he adjusts his position carefully, wedging my legs apart.

Until he can push between them.

He's hard beneath his sweatpants, and he feels strange somehow too. But as he situates himself against me, he rocks his hips forward, pressing his length to my core.

My chest catches in a tiny gasp.

His lips peel back again in a dark grin. "Mine." A long, forked tongue slips from between his jagged teeth to lick along the side of my neck. He inhales again, sharply like he's drawing my scent deep into his lungs, and he repeats in a growl. *"Mine..."*

He rocks his hips forward a second time, rubbing the length of his hard cock against my sweatpants and panties, massaging my clit beneath them.

And fuck... I like it.

I want more.

His eyes widen lasciviously, as if he can tell where my thoughts are going. "Give me mine," he growls.

"Puck..." Phineas warns. "She doesn't have to do anything she doesn't want—"

The Hyde snarls at him, both eyes snapping up to Phineas. "Wants us like this."

Both Zeb and Phineas look at me. "Is that true?" Zeb asks.

Another growl comes from Puck. His grip releases my wrists, but only so he can yank one of my hands down and shove it into his pants.

My fingers wrap around his cock.

His ridged, curved, entirely-too-strange-to-be-human... cock.

My pussy throbs, and I know I'm wet as hell all over again. Creepy is practically throwing a party inside me, desperate to come out and play with the hot, psychotic Hyde who clearly wants to fuck us.

Gods help me, I'm pretty sure I'm on board with that too.

Creepy cheers inside my head. I'm the one in control of our body right now, so I can go first. But after I get fucked by all the guys' deranged, sexy Hydes, it's going to be her turn to play.

A breath leaves me at her proposal. All hell's going to break loose if that happens, but I also know it's that or she tries to take control right now.

Gods, I hope these guys have good insurance.

Grinning like he can see where my thoughts are going, Puck holds my wrist tightly and strokes my hand up and down his ridged cock. "Give this to you. Make you get all creamy and wet around me until you scream."

A growl leaves Phineas, a shudder rolling through him, and he turns away like he's fighting to retain control.

"Mabel?" Urgency fills Zeb's voice.

I swallow hard, and it takes me a moment before I can find my voice. "It's okay." I nod and admit the truth. "I want all of you like this too."

Phineas turns sharply, stalking a few steps closer with his eyes trained on me. I can see wildness to his gaze, hinting his Hyde is close to the surface even if it hasn't broken through yet. "You need to know." His voice is deeper with the rumble of a growl. "The Hydes... they may do or say things that seem a bit strange."

I tense. "Strange?"

"Such as wanting to breed you."

Well, if *that's* not a bucket of cold water on the situation.

Puck snarls at Phineas like he's mad the Jekyll brought it up. "*My* Mabel."

I ignore that as my heart races and my mind does too. "Well, I-I'm on birth control, so..." Shit, I don't know what to say.

Phineas just nods. "Good girl. Anything that happens will always be your choice. And if our Hydes don't agree with that—" He flashes me a grin. "Punch Beastly on his nose. It should startle him, and I'll come back."

Puck growls like he doesn't like the idea of any of us being interrupted.

"You show her respect, Puck," Phineas replies sharply.

The Hyde gives him a surly look. "Always respect." He turns back to me, muttering, "Growly Jekyll's no fun."

He bends down and nuzzles my cheek, rubbing himself against me. My insides melt toward liquid.

Watching us, a shudder rolls through Zeb, like he's fighting to stay in control while hunger flares in his gaze. "Promise me," he presses like he needs to be certain. "You're *sure* you want the Hydes?"

I nod.

Victory fills Puck's expression. "Mine first."

He moves fast, his sharp nails shredding my sweatpants away and taking my underwear with them. My t-shirt is next, sliced to pieces and then ripped aside, and shivers roll through me when the blades of his fingernails graze me without ever breaking my skin.

Puck hums with satisfaction, his wild, electric-blue eyes rolling in different directions, both raking over me as I lie naked on the floor before them all. "Yes. Mine."

He rips off his sweatpants, and my eyes widen. He really does have a cock with ridges on all sides. It's pale but darkened by inky blue skin on every crest. He's long, and his base is thicker than his pointed tip, as if he's been designed to stretch me and hit me deeply with every thrust.

Holy *gods*...

Lightning fast, he's back between my legs and slams his cock into my pussy.

I arch my back with a cry of shock and pleasure.

He's huge, yes, but he's hitting me just right with that strange curve of his cock. When he eases out and then drives himself back into me, his ridges thrum against my muscles, sending pulses of pleasure radiating through my veins and amping up the sensation of him penetrating me.

I grab his ass and moan in spite of myself.

Puck chuckles, his voice low and hungry with something so devilish in the sound. "Mabel. My belle. My soft, *wet* belle. Gonna fill up your sexy pussy. Make you drip with my cum."

Gods save me, Huck's Hyde talks dirty.

He moves suddenly, hefting me upright. My legs wrap around his hips, and I'm higher in the air than I would be if he was in his Jekyll form, given how tall Puck is. His bony hips dig into my thighs, but the angle only serves to pull me tighter against him.

And bury his cock deeper in me.

His sharp nails rest against my ass, sending a thrill through me. At any moment, he could draw blood and somehow, that only makes this more intoxicating.

I'm fucked in the head, I realize, and not just because I have a Hyde in my mind who's currently riding high on having this mad creature thrust himself into us. I can't be normal if I think it's hot that one wrong move could skewer me in an entirely un-cock-like fashion.

Puck twists his long tongue up my neck and around the shell of my ear, and my eyes roll back.

Who needs normal anyway?

My pussy flutters around him as every jerk of his hips drives his cock into me so deep, I'm seeing stars. His deathly pale skin is cold against my breasts, a startling counterpoint to my own warm skin that somehow keeps me wholly focused on him. There's something wild about being with him, like I'm fucking an insane grim reaper or Death himself.

His nails prick my skin, sharp little bites of pain that I know aren't an accident. Not with how he's grinning at me. But the sensation sends my eyes flying wide as a powerful wave of need and pleasure swells in me, poised to crash down.

"Come, my belle," he growls at me.

I cry out, my whole body going tense around him as I come hard as if on command. He thrusts harder, driving his sharp hips into me and making me cling to his bony shoulders.

A wild noise escapes him as his cock shoots hot cum into me, and he grinds me into his hips as if to drive his release even deeper. "Mine," he growls.

I cling to him, my heart still pounding.

Puck holds me for a moment, one of his long-fingered hands running up and down my spine, and then he chuckles, the sound dark and devilish. The pain from the pinpricks on my ass is already fading, leaving only the shuddering aftershocks of all he did to me.

But then he leans to the side a bit and says to someone behind me, "Should give her more."

Oh gods, these men are going to have me unconscious for days from all the orgasms.

Creepy *definitely* doesn't think that's a bad thing.

I twist, attempting to figure out which of the guys he's talking to, but then Phineas is there.

Except it's not Phineas. It's his Hyde. He's seven feet tall and covered in fur. His tail whips behind him and clouds of green vapor rise around his muzzle as he sniffs in my scent.

"Beastly fucks you now too," Puck says to me with approval.

Phineas's Hyde growls, sounding every bit as wild as his name, and it sends an exhilarating shiver of fear straight back to some primal part of my mind.

But that primal part doesn't *just* feel that ancient fear of facing a monster. It's also aroused as hell at the idea of being claimed by the monster, and the combination is confusing and overwhelming all at the same time.

A low chuckle leaves Beastly. Even if he has the head of a wolf, I swear he grins.

Without preamble, he picks me up off Puck's cock, turns me to him, and thrusts himself into me.

Oh, holy *gods*...

I shriek as his thick cock stretches me, and I'm grateful Puck got me off first because I'm not sure I could've taken Beastly without being at least somewhat relaxed already. Instinctively, I wrap my legs around him too and grip his furry back, clinging to him for dear life as he rocks his hips back and then forward again, pulling out and then thrusting into me. His body is so much bigger than mine, I'm just pressed to his chest with his massive arms holding me in place, but the position means I hear and feel the thrum of satisfaction and approval that goes through his chest as he buries himself deep in me. It catches on a grunt of pleasure and then returns as he drives himself into me again.

I flush warm with pride that I'm doing this to him. That Phineas's Hyde wants this as much as his Jekyll side did.

Beastly's massive, clawed hands take my sides. He leans me back, supporting me as firmly as if I were lying on a hammock, so that he can see me in front of him while he controls how hard he drives himself into me.

Something teases at my ass, and I look down sharply to see his tail has curved around his side. The long fur at the end brushes between my cheeks, adding shivers of pleasure to what he's already doing.

Gods, these Hydes...

I tighten my legs around him, returning my gaze to his wolfish face. The mist still rises from him in huffs, but the vibrant green liquid I'd originally seen when he first shifted for me earlier now hovers around his fangs.

A tiny bit of worry nibbles at my arousal. Is that venom? Will it poison me if it drops onto my skin?

Beastly lets out a low growl, and my eyes snap back to his. That glint is back in his gaze. I swear he grins again.

Gods, the devil himself couldn't look more devious than these Hydes.

Leaning forward a bit, Beastly lets some of the green, viscous liquid drip from his fangs onto my abdomen.

It hits my skin and I come. Hard and fast, like I've been hit by the two-by-four of an orgasm. The blinding wave of pleasure rockets through me, blasting my mind to pieces while I arch my back in his grasp.

Sweet *gods*...

Orgasm after orgasm crashes into me in rapid succession as he drips that amazing green liquid onto my skin, making me writhe and buck and moan like a wild thing in his grip. Just when I think I can't take anymore, he begins thrusting into me harder, holding me while my body sags. His cock feels even bigger in my pussy now. I don't know how it's possible. But it makes me gasp and rock as I try to match his pace even though my body feels made of putty.

He grunts one final time and slams his hips into me. I swear his cock stretches me even wider than before, just to the border of being seriously painful.

I'm delirious with the afterglow of everything he's done. Holding me in place, Beastly stops moving, but I feel him pulsing inside me, pumping his cum into my body. Breathless, I lie in his grip, reeling.

But he doesn't pull away as the seconds tick past, and his cock still feels huge inside me. I hesitate, not sure what to say, but Puck seems to read my expression.

"Knotted you," he says, running his fingers along my side and making me shudder all over again. "Keeps his cum inside you to breed you." His hand swirls over my middle like he's imagining little Jekylls and Hydes growing inside me.

I swallow hard. So that's what Phineas was talking about. His Hyde and what it wanted.

What Puck wants too, from the look of it.

"We're not breeding right now," I tell them.

A pout flashes over Puck's face, but Beastly only pulls my hips tighter against him, growling as he grinds my clit against his body.

Creepy tingles through my skin. She doesn't mind the idea of having a family with these Hydes. But she won't have them thinking *they* get to decide when that happens.

"Not... now," I repeat, and her voice carries through mine.

Beastly meets my eyes again, and then he draws me upright so I'm against his chest. His knot is still inside me, but after a moment, it's deflated enough that it doesn't hurt when he pulls me off of his cock. Holding me close like I'm precious to him, he nuzzles my head with the underside of his massive jaw.

"Someday," he rumbles.

I blink. I didn't know he could speak in this form.

He runs his hands up and down my back like he's cuddling me, and it makes some of my tension melt. Hydes don't always understand the intricacies of life.

They're fairly straightforward about everything, even if their version of logic doesn't always make sense to anyone else.

So of course Beastly and Puck don't see how complicated this all actually is.

As if proving my thoughts right, Puck turns, grinning. "Ghastly next."

I look over my shoulder to find Zeb still in his Jekyll form several feet away. His hard cock is noticeable in his pants, but he hasn't taken off any clothes or shifted at all.

I give him a confused look.

He hesitates, that same uncertainty on his face that I saw when he and the others first revealed their Hydes to me. Like for some reason he's wondering if I'll run away, even now. "I have something special planned for you, beautiful. If you'll trust me, that is."

I'm baffled. "I trust you."

Even though he grins, that worried look still isn't fully gone. "Okay. If you feel even a little bit uncomfortable, though, you tell me to stop, understand? This is important. Promise me?"

I nod warily. "I promise."

He nods back, looking a touch relieved. "Can you stand up? It'd be best if we started with you—"

The front door explodes.

Ballistic pieces of wood shred the air, but Beastly moves instantly, twisting away with incredible speed to cover me. Past his arm, I spot a canister tumbling into the living room.

He presses my face to his furry chest as another explosion, this time of light and sound, suddenly rips through the room.

Flash-bang, I think in shock, all my senses jangling. Holy shit, that was a flash-bang. I've seen them in movies.

Hollywood doesn't do them justice.

But Beastly's quick reaction means my eyes aren't as dazed as my ears, and when I look up again, smoke is pouring from a second canister, sending clouds of it billowing up to choke the room.

As quickly as he shielded me, Beastly is gone.

I cough, pushing away from the ground. My hearing is muffled, but I make out the sound of shouting. Crashing. Beastly appears briefly through the smoke, a black-clad intruder held aloft in his grip. Tentacles thrash in the shadows as Zeb's Hyde, Ghastly, rips away anyone who tries to leave the smoke to reach me. Puck launches into the fray, his long fingers and claws extended. Screams follow and blood sprays from amid the clouds of smoke to splatter across the carpet.

Creepy surges up. We're buck-fricking-naked and dripping cum, but she doesn't care. She wants to fight. To help. To devour these intruders who think they can hurt our Jekylls and Hydes.

Sounds good to me.

I take a breath, ready to release my hold on her.

A small object whips out of the smoke, striking my neck before I'm done shifting or can move out of the way. My black-nailed hand rises, smacking at it and finding a dart.

It's bigger than the one the traders used before. It's attached to a vial that's only got a tiny amount of bluish liquid still inside it.

Ghastly tumbles out of the smoke and crashes to the ground ahead of me, his tentacles limp on the floor. Beastly howls, but I see him stagger in the fog. Puck is a shadowy figure in the smoke and he leaps toward something farther on that I can't see.

But then he stumbles back too. He tries to rally, charging forward again, and popping noises penetrate the thick cotton in my ears.

He lurches.

They shot him. Oh gods, they shot Puck, not with tranqs but with bullets from an actual fucking gun.

Creepy screams in rage and I do too. I lunge toward our Hyde, the shift rushing through me.

But another dart hits us, sending a second flood of tranquilizer into our veins. The effect is too strong and the darkness is too fast, and before Creepy or I make it another step, the combination sends us tumbling into oblivion.

CHAPTER 14

ZEB

The world returns in fits and starts, flashing scenes that make Ghastly want to rip our enemies apart, except we can't escape the darkness in order to find them. People surround us only to vanish again. A rumbling sound fills our ears and a metal wall is in our face, and then both are gone. Bright lights flash. Glaring lights. Lights that make me want to recoil because they stab like needles in my eyes. My thoughts blur with Ghastly's, and half the time, I can't tell who is in control of our body.

And then I wake up.

Screeching sounds fill the air, erratic and interrupted by short bursts of a bug-zapper type of buzzing. Something clammy presses against my cheek, and it isn't until my eyes focus that I see I'm lying on a rubbery floor with metal bars ahead. My entire body aches, from my scalp to my toes to my teeth, but I'm the one in control for the moment. Ghastly is still groggy inside my mind.

And then memory starts to return.

Mabel.

A flood of adrenaline and rage roars through my veins, propelling me to my feet.

I only make it halfway before my legs give out.

Crashing to my knees, I catch myself with an arm that's stained green and purple like the hue of Ghastly's tentacles. I ignore it, though. My eyes dart around the room, my vision blending with Ghastly's to make the scene warp in a dizzying way.

But she's not here.

And the rest is hell.

I'm inside a cage. Beastly lies in another one across the room, motionless, and I'm frozen for the moment it takes me to spot how—thank the gods—his chest is still rising and falling. He's my family, and Huck and Puck are too, every bit as much as my parents and siblings and hopefully Mabel someday. If whoever grabbed us had killed him...

I shudder, pushing that nightmare aside. We're in some kind of loading dock, complete with large rolling doors to my left and markings on the floor to caution workers not to get too close. There's a pair of double doors to my right that look industrial too, but more like they lead into a building, while blindingly bright lights glare down from overhead, offering nowhere to hide.

Several yards to the right of Beastly's cage, Puck is locked up as well, and he's obviously the source of the screeching I heard when I woke up. Like a deranged hornet in a box, he's ricocheting madly off metal bars that jolt him with electricity every time he hits them. Scrapes mar the concrete floor where his efforts have made the cage shift across the ground. Bloodstained bandages are taped haphazardly to the majority of his bullet wounds, though a few gauzy scraps lie scattered on the ground like he ripped them off in his rage. Trails of dried blood crisscross his deathly pale skin, but the wounds themselves have long since closed, joining the pockmarks of old burns and jagged scars from his past. He and Huck can take a hell of a beating before they go down—a fact the sick bastard who kept him like a toy used to his advantage countless times.

But right now, the new cage and the fact Mabel is gone have obviously driven Puck past the limit of whatever rationality he still possessed. And considering who I suspect our captors might be, what they'll do to him if he doesn't calm down makes panic begin pounding like a drum in the back of my mind.

"Puck." I start to grab the bars and then retreat at the buzz of electricity there. "Puck!"

The Hyde can't hear me. He's too far gone.

Ghastly rises up, reacting to my fear and Puck's alike, and it's all I can do to wrestle him back down. Yes, this is bad. It's so fucking bad that, if we make it out of here, I'm definitely going to have nightmares. But we have to be smart. Make a plan. Keep our heads so that we *do* get out, and so that we can fucking butcher the bastards who thought they could take Mabel from us.

Ghastly recedes. Not much, but enough that I can think beyond keeping him contained.

There's no doubt in my mind traders are behind this. The fact they've got us here, in a motherfucking loading dock, only reinforces that suspicion. But I won't let myself believe they've taken Mabel away already. No, she'll be here, maybe in a different room, but here.

Which means we'll find her. Gut anyone who touched her. And make sure we never let anyone near her again.

Puck flings himself full-body at the bars, screaming as they burn him.

But first things first. "Puck!"

Still nothing. But in his cage, Beastly stirs, pushing up from the ground and growling like the monster he is.

Puck scrambles up to fling himself at the bars again.

"Dammit, Puck!" I shout. "Stop!"

He's not listening.

"Puck, Mabel needs you to calm down *right now*!"

The Hyde freezes, his eyes snapping to me. "My belle."

Thank the gods...

"You'll get your chance to kill the ones who took your belle, but only if you let them get close, understand? So you have to stay calm."

Puck starts shaking, but his enormous eyes don't leave me. There's a trace of rationality in his gaze now. Beastly's too. It's not sanity because the Hydes have never been sane, but I can see a focused intensity that shows their minds have started working past their rage and fear again.

And sure, it's the kind of focused intensity that would string the traders' teeth into a necklace, but I'll take what I can get.

Ghastly mutters about pretty tooth necklaces for Mabel. I ignore him.

"Did you see where they took her?" I ask Puck.

The Hyde lifts one long arm and points his knife-like finger toward the door on the righthand side of the room.

Relief makes air rush from my chest. She's here, then. I can't let myself imagine what they might be doing to her—I'll lose control of Ghastly if I consider that for too long—but she's here and that's a start.

"Okay, good. Now, did you see how they control these cages? Is there a key or a code or—"

The double doors open.

Six guys walk in dressed in khakis like zookeepers. Ghastly snarls in my mind at the pretense, the arrogance. It's on purpose, I know. A show to intimidate us and to create a sense of danger and wildness for buyers too.

And it probably means they're going to hold an auction soon. Maybe not here, not if we're in the fucking loading dock, but somewhere, and they want the buyers to feel like they're getting rare animals.

Not living sentient beings with hopes and dreams and thoughts of their own, no. Never that.

Just rare animals, all without the trouble of traveling to far-off lands or actually risking anything.

Ghastly shivers through my skin, wanting to show them just how *wild* we can be, and I take a breath, reminding him that we need to stay calm. Need to stay focused.

We can't kill them all, not yet. We need to know where Mabel is first.

And we need to get out of these fucking cages.

"I see one of you is trying to pretend to look human," one of the men says, his tone bored. From the way the others are reacting to him, I'm guessing he's the sick fucker in charge. "You really do enjoy that game, don't you? As if you could hide what you are."

"Where is she?" I demand.

The man smirks. "Only something like you freaks would want a hideous cunt like that."

It gets harder to control Ghastly—and harder to want to try. But we have to be smart. We have to be...

Gods, I'll make them eat their own tongues.

The guy in charge saunters up to the cage. "Don't you worry about your little freak. Our crew's keeping her entertained. By the time we're done, she won't even remember you."

Puck screams, his voice like knives grating over metal. Beastly roars, grabbing the bars and howling when the electricity burns him. The smell of scorched fur joins the stench of concrete and sweat in the air.

I stay quiet, my body shaking all over, while

Ghastly seethes beneath my skin, cataloging all of the ways he'll make these men pay for touching her.

I'm on board with each and every one.

"She's your mate, isn't she?" the man continues. "All of you, sharing the same bitch. Couldn't find anyone else to touch your cocks, eh?" He smirks as his buddies come closer, cattle prods in their hands. "You want to know how she's begging for it? How she's on the ground like an animal for us? Or how about what her new owner will do once we sell her?"

Everything Huck suffered, everything I've seen over and over again in all these years of rescuing people from the traders, flashes through my mind in an instant.

I can't keep Ghastly under control now.

I don't even try.

The shift takes me fast. My vision blurs into Ghastly's, seeing more than my Jekyll eyes ever could. My back arches as tentacles burst from my skin, my spine, my shoulders. At lightning speed, the powerful limbs shoot past the bars in all directions.

Because that man was a fool. His buddies too.

They got too close.

Ghastly's tentacles whip around their throats, round and round while their fingers pry at his flesh. He squeezes down, making their faces darken with panic and trapped blood.

But it's not choking them that either of us has in mind.

Ghastly's true gift, the darkest side of it, flows through his skin and out into the suckers now attached to their throats.

Images flash through our mind. Supernaturals crying. Screaming. Begging and pleading and whimpering. Mothers with their children being ripped away. Fathers flinging themselves at the bars just like Puck and Beastly did, fighting desperately to reach their loved ones.

Failing every time.

From the back of Ghastly's mind, I watch as my Hyde's madness—*our* madness—pours like burning lava into the traders' brains. When we want to be, the two of us are monsters in every sense of the word, but my parents long since taught me that isn't a bad thing.

Sometimes, it takes a monster to stop the monsters.

Sometimes, a monster is the only kind of good guy the world gets.

Pure insanity rolls inexorably across the traders' brains, melting their thoughts, their wills, their identities, and their sick, twisted dreams. And they can't withstand it. In the end, they were never brave or strong. They weren't powerful, not really.

They're cowards who feed on fear and who hurt others because they can.

And they can't survive something like me.

Their bodies begin to seize and shake as their brains overheat and turn to mush. Blood vessels burst in their eyes and noses from the strain, sending red rivers streaming down. They gibber and they snap, breaking their teeth but still managing to bite off their own tongues with the jagged remnants. Choking on both, they spasm and blubber while their bowels fail and the reek of shit and piss fill the air.

Ghastly grins, and deep in his mind, I do too. Like hell these fuckers will ever hurt anyone again.

Lightning suddenly erupts from the bars so powerfully, it's like the whole damn cage has become a box of electricity. Howling, Ghastly crashes backward. The smell of burned flesh chokes me, and from the agony, I'm guessing it's probably ours.

I shudder. I'm still in the back of his mind, Ghastly holding prominence but only barely.

What the *fuck*?

Ghastly's eyes flash around the room while he shoves up from the ground on tentacles that quiver with residual shocks. The bastards lie on the concrete, reduced to vegetables with bodies that will probably give up on living soon. Across the room, Beastly growls and Puck grins madly, both of them thoroughly approving of what Ghastly did.

"Well, that's unfortunate."

Ghastly's eyes snap to the side.

By the double doors, and damnably beyond tentacles' reach, a man in a suit stands, idly tapping something into a tablet computer in his hand. "We were hoping you would go over well with the Lovecraft enthusiasts."

A rattling growl leaves Ghastly's chest.

The man just sighs, looking back up at us. "Oh well."

He motions to a redheaded woman beside him. Like the other sick fucks in this place, she's wearing khakis. She even has a pith helmet on her head like she's about to go on a gods-damned safari, and it makes me sick.

She stalks closer and then lifts a gun, nothing but ice in her eyes. Ghastly reacts instantly, sending his tentacles shooting through the bars at her.

But she gets her shot off first.

Three darts strike Ghastly's chest, clustered tightly above his heart. Ghastly staggers backward, numbness sweeping his limbs and tentacles.

I try to make him shift back. To give me control. But the drug is messing with me, making my thoughts muzzy. My sense of my body slips through my fingers like smoke.

Ghastly crashes down to his knees.

The suit-clad man walks closer, the woman at his side still holding her gun at the ready. "We already have buyers lined up for you and your little friends. Jekylls and Hydes are a rare commodity, and our clients will pay top dollar to acquire you. But be that as it may, some of you are simply too dangerous to let live. We can't let the brains of our buyers melt, after all. Bad for business."

The sedative makes the world swirl. Ghastly's cheek hits the floor as our muscles give out.

"But that doesn't mean we don't have use for you. Or, rather, that our military contractor friends don't."

Through the fading blur of the room, I see the man twitch his chin at me. While the woman keeps her gun level, another man comes forward. The knife in his fist glints like a star in the encroaching darkness.

From far away, I hear Beastly roar. Hear Puck scream in rage.

But I can't even move.

"If we can't sell the monster," the first guy says. "We can still make use of its parts."

ICE CREAM
Cookies
CANDY
Candy
Tasty
sing aLong

CHAPTER 15

CREEPY MABEL

The thick dark thinks it can hold me.

I'll kill it too.

I thrash and twist, screaming against the muffling blanket of nothingness between me and my body. It's pinning me down, keeping me from reaching my Hydes and killing the ones who hurt them. I'll feed it back to itself in bloody pieces if it doesn't stop soon.

The darkness gets scared. Retreats and grows thin because it knows I'll be victorious.

Nothing gets between me and my Hydes.

I snarl again, determined to make it fade entirely.

My voice comes out as a grumbly groan, but it's enough. The darkness does what I want and goes away.

But it leaves pain behind.

My eyes burn when I open them. My limbs ache like someone stomped on every joint and bone. I snarl again, and even though my throat scratches like it's full of thorns and stones, the sound is clearer.

The pain recedes a bit. Good. It should be scared of me too.

I blink and scan my surroundings, my rage growing. Bars. I'm surrounded by a circle of metal bars. They're thicker than my wrist and they go into the concrete ground like they've been impaled there. Over my head, they bend inward until they meet in the middle.

A cage. Big enough to hold a dragon and with stains on the concrete like blood that didn't wash fully away.

I push to my feet, snarling so fiercely it sounds like a scream.

Something clanks on my wrist. I look down.

I'm dressed again. I shouldn't be. The other was naked when those evil people attacked us. Red cotton covers me now, pants and a V-neck shirt like an outfit I've seen on nurses, but in the color of blood. I don't mind that last part, but I'm furious someone dared to touch us.

And they gave us jewelry too. A thick bracelet

hangs on my left wrist. It's at least two inches wide, made of nearly solid metal but with a groove in its side like someone carved a chunk out of it all the way around. A thinner band of metal rests in the groove, gold while the rest of the metal is silver, and when I move, it glints weirdly like the silver portions are covered in an oil slick.

I wrap my fingers around it and tug, but nothing happens. The metal feels funny, though. All buzzy against my hand like a live wire, but I don't know why.

My eyes go to the room beyond the cage again. Everything is still. My Hydes aren't here. I can't hear them either, not my Beastly or my Ghastly or…

Memory flashes behind my eyes. My Puck. They shot my Puck.

A screech escapes me, my body trembling with rage. My gaze rakes the room, searching for any sign of where my Hydes have gone, but there's nothing. Past the bars, the concrete floor goes down several steps on all sides and then continues until it reaches a ring of haphazardly placed chairs, like ones for an audience, except no one put them all away when that audience was gone.

Gritting my teeth against the way my body aches, I turn a tight circle. I can't even tell where the gate on the cage is located, but the room beyond it has a door past the chairs. It's made of dark wood, ornate and polished, and there's a keypad beside it with a little red light glowing on top. Above the door, a gallery with more misplaced chairs stretches across that side of the room, as if providing more places for the audience to sit. Besides the abandoned chairs, I can't see much past the short wooden wall and brass railing on top of it.

My eyes narrow. The other is asleep as always, but I remember her sneaky friends telling her about places like this. This is a place where traders bring their captives. A place where they put them on display and sell them to the highest bidder, like those rich people in that movie where the scientists made dinosaurs come back again.

In that movie, all the rich people got eaten.

I like this plan.

Grinning, I stalk toward the bars. I can flicker between them. No stupid cage is going to hold me. And when I find the ones who took me, who shot my Puck...

I blink out of sight and dart between the bars.

Or try to.

Electricity surges through me like I've stepped into a lightning bolt. I crash back to the concrete, screaming with pain while my body spasms from the residual shocks.

Slow clapping sounds push past the ringing in my ears. I pry my eyes open as the pain dulls.

A man walks toward me, the door swinging shut behind him. I get a glimpse of a long hallway with more doors and golden lights, and then it's gone, leaving only me and him and a cage that bites.

"We know about your little power, Hyde," the man says, smiling. Ordinarily, I'd appreciate that the expression looks like a shark, except this shark is between me and my Hydes and obviously knew about the cage that could hurt me.

I can kill sharks too.

Pushing to my feet again, I fight the way my body wants to wobble as I glare down at him. He's wearing a black suit and a pale-brown shirt with a dark tie that has little gold symbols on it that match the keychain of the man I killed days ago. His hair is gray and his skin has that pale look white businessmen get from spending too much time in the office, but he still moves easily, like part of that time in the office is at the company gym.

He stops a few yards shy of the cage, tapping something briefly on his phone and then lifting the device so its underside is pointed at me. A click sounds like a camera shutter, and then he tucks the phone away. "Photos," he says calmly. "For the marketing material."

I'll pick every one of his muscles apart.

"The accessory we've given you will suppress any other powers you might have." He nods toward the bracelet. "We can get to the details on whatever those might be later. The buyers will surely want to know, plus it could raise our opening price. But in the meantime, let's get the preliminaries out of the way." His brow rises while he regards me. "Can you speak?"

I'll make him eat his own liver.

The man waits and then sighs like my silence is disappointing but doesn't really matter either way. "I suppose you're wondering how we found you. Suffice it to say you subhumans really aren't nearly as clever as you think you are. We tracked you after you killed one of our members a few days back, but several of our crew got a little ahead of themselves and burned your house down before we could acquire you. We could have lost you then, but thankfully, your security detail featured a few individuals we've had on our radar for a while, not that they or whatever agency they work for knows that. Once we spotted them, it wasn't difficult to conclude a target of value was likely nearby.

Imagine our satisfaction when that turned out to be you and your unusual companions."

He scoffs to himself as if something is ironically amusing. "*Companions.* Is that the word you would use? Or are those three creatures your 'mates'? Such a disgusting term—at least as you subhumans use it. But then, you're all barely better than wild animals who can speak, so I suppose it makes sense you would find appeal in such a word."

I quiver, my rage surging higher. "Hurt my friends. This is how you end."

His brow rises. "You rhyme. How adorable."

"Ate your buddy," I warn. "Eat you happily."

"Well, now that's a sloppier rhyme, don't you think? Buddy. Happily." He shrugs. "No matter. The buyers will love that little trick. Perhaps they'll want you as entertainment for their guests. Like a poet. Edgar Allan Poe in a cage." Chuckling to himself, he takes out his phone again, tapping it briefly like he's typing in notes.

Agonized screams rise in the distance. My eyes snap from the man to the door.

My Hydes. Someone is hurting them.

Rage floods me, and I lunge toward the bars, stopping just shy of the metal. Electricity tingles on my skin in savage little bites that warn of more if I come any closer.

Sighing, the man casts a brief glance toward the sound and then returns his attention to me. "I'm afraid not all your *mates* are as suitable for sale in their current state as you are. But the market for Hyde organs is... well, lucrative, considering how rare it is to capture *one* of you, let alone four."

Lightning bites at me as I flinch forward, my fingers curling and my nails digging into my palms. This close to the bars, I can see the dead twisting around him, swirling through the air. Their forms are faint, though. More like a heat mirage than the misty shapes I normally see.

My gaze drops to the buzzy bracelet. It would suppress me, he said. Stop what I can do.

I can't flicker. I can't reach the one who needs to die. I can barely see the dead—and just *seeing* them is useless anyway.

But when those other dead gave my Puck and Huck nightmares...

I tremble. I don't command the dead. I see and hear them, that's all. But when I needed to protect my Hyde and Jekyll from the ghosts tormenting them, that changed.

Except... the other was the one who was awake when that happened, not me.

In my head, the other stirs as if hearing my thought, and I freeze, shocked. She's always asleep when I'm awake. She wants it that way. It protects her from what I do to make the world safe, because if she's awake, she tries to stop me. What I do scares her.

But now she's waking. She's still scared, but she doesn't want to sleep, not anymore.

Not when someone is hurting our men.

Pink energy tangles inside me, like a blush on the night sky that promises sunrise.

More cries rise in the distance. Howls that make me want to fling myself at the bars, pain and electricity be damned.

I can't lose my Beastly or my Ghastly or my Puck. I just found them, and we *need* each other. *I* need them. I was so alone before. The other and I both were, even if she never wanted to think about it. And once we found our Jekylls and our Hydes, that changed.

The pink glow of sunrise spreads in my veins. The other's reassurance comes with it, like the comforting thoughts she sends when I'm frightened. Because she loves me and protects me too, even if I make her scared sometimes.

"Would you care to tell me your name?" the man

asks idly, like my Hydes aren't shrieking in the distance. "Or should I just make one up for you?"

Her comfort turns to resolve. We won't lose them now.

We're going to fight.

Quivers of determination make my hair shake like a stringy black curtain. Make my hand curl into a fist around the bracelet too. The metal is cold against my skin, a chilly bite on the edge of pain that grows stronger with the glow of the other's power spreading through me.

Baring my teeth, I lift my eyes to where the man in the suit stands. He's looking at his phone again.

I growl.

He glances up, a calmly curious expression on his face. "Poe-lina?" He shakes his head at himself. "No, that's too Thumbelina and you don't look enough like a fairy to make that sell. Emily, perhaps. Like Emily Dickinson. You do have that tragically gothic aesthetic going. Perhaps if we put you in a white nightgown. Buyers might find the allusion amusing."

"Creepy."

His brow twitches up. "Your name is 'Creepy'?" He scoffs like I've said something ridiculous.

My fingers close tighter around the bracelet, and my muscles strain as I pull on it. "They call me Creepy

Mabel. Maybe you think that's not so nice. But you just hurt my mates, *you ass*, so now it's time to end your life."

He regards me indulgently. "You're hardly in a position, *Creepy*, to threaten—"

"Kill him," I hiss at the dead.

The heat shimmers pause in their swirling, and then every one of them quivers strangely in the air. I can barely see the vaguest hints of their presence, yet I know—just *know*—they've turned to look at me.

My grip strains harder on the bracelet and my body trembles with fury as I reach for every scrap of power I can still feel in my veins past the bracelet's suppressing force.

My eyes never leave the dead.

Chuckling, the man continues in his indulgent tone. "What did you say?"

So many dead. So many innocent lives destroyed. He's nothing but one among countless other predators in the world, but in this moment, that doesn't matter.

He's the only one in this room.

"The buyers won't tolerate obstinance," the man says, "so you'll answer when I speak. What did you—"

"Kill him!"

Confusion flickers in his amused expression. He starts to look around theatrically.

But the dead are hungry for their revenge.

The heat shimmers begin to swirl again, spiraling around him even though he can't see them at all. But then far-off screams whisper through the room, like distant sounds carried on a wind.

The man's amused expression melts into confusion and then true alarm.

He taps something quickly on his phone and then aims the device at me like it's a weapon.

The bracelet suddenly flares hot on my wrist like the metal is on fire.

I shriek, collapsing to the ground and clawing at it, but I can't break it away. *"Kill him!"*

Faster and faster, the dead swirl. Their screams grow louder like a freight train racing toward us.

The man lurches as one of the heat shimmers slashes at him. The sleeve of his suit jacket shreds like claws have torn through it, and blood seeps into the edges of the torn fabric.

Victorious cries join the screams of the dead. The pain surging through me fades as the man's device goes flying from his grasp. Again, he lurches as bloody scratches suddenly slice across his cheek. His forehead. His arm. His neck.

Eyes wide, he stares at me as he retreats toward the door.

I push back to my feet. "Don't let him go," I growl.

The dead descend on him as one. He screams as his suit shreds and his blood splatters. Wildly, he thrashes under the assault of things he can't see.

I grin.

In only moments, nothing remains of him that hasn't been sliced or torn. The heat shimmers rise from his mangled corpse, but they don't drift upward into light like they always have.

They float toward me.

I tense, taking a step back warily. What's this? I helped free them. Are they going to come after me too?

They reach the bars and hover beyond the cage. I wait, not sure what to think. Is the biting electricity holding them back? Do I have the nasty trader to thank for why they're not attacking me?

The heat shimmers pass through the gaps between the bars, and suddenly, they're not heat shimmers anymore. Like people stepping from behind a curtain, they transform as they pass the bars, not becoming swirls of mist but instead ghostly figures, their bodies foggy white and partially see-through.

I resist the urge to snarl at them, if only because they're making me worried. There's a woman with long hair and pointed ears in a flowing dress. Another in overalls with short hair and wide, large eyes. Several men in everything from jeans and t-shirts to construc-tion worker clothes.

And children.

I tremble at the sight of the little ones, wishing I could bring that evil man back and kill him all over again just because they're here.

One of the children steps forward. She's wearing a little sundress with flowers that stirs in a breeze I can't feel. Her eyes are huge, even bigger than mine, and they shine like bottomless pools. But her heart-shaped face is kind as she smiles up at me. "Thank you for freeing us."

Reaching out, she wraps her hand around the bracelet.

The metal clicks and falls open, dropping to the ground.

She glances back and one of the older guys in over-alls puts a hand to the bars.

A gate swings open.

My heart pounds, but I stop myself from rushing out to save my men right now. I don't know what the dead want.

I can't risk offending them and ending up like that horrible man.

Turning back to me, the girl's smile falls, and her

shining eyes turn to pools of worry mingled with hope. "There are others. Can you free them too?"

Inside me, the other stirs at the words. She hasn't gone back to sleep even now, and she's not hiding from this anymore.

No, she wants to help. She wants to do what the little girl asks.

Together.

I smile. We are the vengeance and the hope.

We are the ones to whom the dead souls turn.

I hum to myself as I head for the exit. We have work to do.

CHAPTER 16
MABEL

I gasp as between one step and the next, we shift, and suddenly I'm the one in the cage, not Creepy.

But I can still see the dead.

I stop in my tracks, staring at the ghostly figures around me. I've only seen the dead once when Huck was having his nightmare, but they'd been nothing more than mist. I've never been able to see them like Creepy can. Our gifts are different. Like how Ghastly has tentacles and Zeb doesn't. We're not the same creatures, even though we live in the same skin.

Yet now Creepy and I are sharing in a way we never have before, and I think maybe it's not just because we found the others to help us have balance.

It's because of me. Because I stopped pushing her

down, stopped letting myself be pulled under by unconsciousness when she was the one in control of our body.

We're not each other's alter ego anymore. We're Creepy Mabel in truth, not just name.

And she's letting me take control.

Pink light and mist flare around my hands. The energy grows, crackling like lightning around my forearms.

My eyes lift to the room again. If the rest of that asshole's crew are in this building, they almost certainly heard him screaming. So even if the traders are regrouping, they'll be in here soon.

"Will you be okay?" I ask the ghosts around me.

They smile, and the little girl with the heart-shaped face nods. She might be a fae. I can't be sure. But she glances at the others before turning back to me. "We want to help."

My brow climbs. Well, then...

The ghosts pull back, making space as I stride out of the cage. I scan the room while I descend the steps from the elevated platform to the main floor, and I spot a few little black boxes that might be cameras perched up high in the shadows.

So the bad guys could be watching us right now.

Okay.

Bright-pink lightning flies from my hands, lashing out across the room like crackling arrows shooting out around me all at the same time. The devices pop and scatter, blown apart by the blasts and leaving only smoking scorch marks on the walls where they were anchored.

In my head, Creepy smiles.

I do the same. That felt good.

Turning my attention to the little keypad by the door, I lift a hand.

The door bursts open before I can let our magic go.

People in black tactical gear rush into the room, and it's not a stretch to guess they're traders or the crew's security. It's not just the weapons or the fact they're here.

It's the misty spirits hovering above and around them, thrashing like trapped birds that can't break free.

The tactical team levels their guns at me, and the one in the lead shouts, "Get on the ground now!"

Sure.

I smile as I sink to the cold concrete, buying time, and when I speak, Creepy's singsong rattle carries through my voice. "Dead around those I see. Kill the killers and be set free."

Magic shivers through my veins.

Screams break out in the room. I press myself fully to the floor as bullets rake the chairs and walls, fired wildly by the tactical team at the attackers they can't see.

The gunfire trails off. The room stills.

I shove to my feet. My arms are speckled with blood, and my hair is too. Ordinarily, Creepy flickers in and out of view to avoid that, I recall. I should figure out if I can do that too.

But first...

I veer around the pooled blood and the bodies as I head into the hallway. Most of the doors are closed, giving me no clue whether my men are inside.

The ghosts nearest to me glance at each other, and I get the strangest sense they're communicating. But before I can ask, the girl with the heart-shaped face flashes me another smile.

And then they all scatter, drifting through the doors and returning a moment later.

"No one," the girl says.

The other ghosts echo her response.

I thank them and keep moving. More doors turn up nothing, until I round the corner at the end of the hall and hear a scream come from somewhere farther on.

Zeb. I swear that sounded like Zeb.

I run. The ghosts race ahead of me, whipping through doors and then back out, shaking their heads quickly, over and over. I dart past another corner, and then another, running onward through a maze-like building that never seems to end.

Panic starts to grip me. Was this a trick? Were the screams a recording or some other ploy to torment me, when really my men are anywhere but here?

At the end of the hall, the ghost girl dives through and then reappears quickly, her enormous eyes wide. "Here!" She points.

In a blast of pink lightning, my magic takes out the lock. I burst past the door.

It's a large room. Cement floor. Drains every few feet to catch the blood. Industrial lights blaze down, offering nowhere to hide. A truck loading dock is at one end, and a semi has been backed into place with its trailer door open and standing ready.

My men are here too. They're trapped in square cages, but smaller than the one I was held inside and not bolted to the ground either. Cages for transport.

For killing.

Puck is in one, snarling and throwing himself against bars that flare like electric firecrackers every time he makes contact with them. Blood-stained bandages haphazardly cover his bullet wounds like someone only half-heartedly tried to stop the bleeding. Burn marks score his pale skin from head to toe, evidence of how many times he's flung himself into the walls of the cage.

Beastly is wounded too, burns on his sides and chunks of fur missing. He stands in another cage, snarling as he turns this way and that like he's looking for an escape, but he's surrounded by traders with cattle prods in their fists. They're rolling his cage toward the truck.

Ghastly's cage is off to one side. He lies on the ground, not moving. A savage cut mars one of his legs, torn straight through his pants like someone wanted to test how well he handled being sliced and diced. His tentacles lie limp on the cage floor around him, burned in places like they were scorched by electricity.

But one tentacle is missing. The stump seeps black blood where the appendage was sliced away, coating his back in the dark liquid. Dressed in butcher's smocks, three of the traders have his severed tentacle trapped between them. It thrashes of its own accord, but still they carry it toward a glass case like a science experiment they intend to put on display.

I scream.

The dead with me race at the traders, while the ghosts hovering around the bastards pause.

There are so many dead surrounding them that it's hard to distinguish one from the other. But at my scream, pink smoke and lightning surge around me, and all those dead turn too, as if they suddenly are energized.

And then they attack.

Traders scream and try to run. They grab for weapons, but there's nothing to shoot. Nothing to slash their knives at or attack at all.

Some of them turn and rush at me.

They don't make it more than a few steps. The dead tear into them, knocking them to the ground and ripping at the traders as they scream. Others try to make a break for the door to escape the carnage, only to be driven back by the dead waiting there. I stride through the chaos quickly, heading for Ghastly and Zeb's cage, and the ghost girl and several others come with me.

"Ghastly?" I wait but he doesn't move. "Zeb? Please, answer me."

Nothing.

I lash out at the lock with my lightning. Before it even reaches the metal, the energy breaks apart, pink electricity snarling over the bars but changing nothing, like it can't get inside.

Within the cage, Ghastly doesn't stir.

Desperate, I turn to the ghosts. "Can you open it?"

The ghost girl doesn't waste a second, instantly shattering the lock on the door. I want to lunge forward to reach Ghastly right now, but I make myself pause long enough to check that the bars don't burn when I go near them.

But like the cage I was in, the defenses on this one seem to have died when the gate opened.

I rush inside. "Ghastly." I press my fingers to his neck and then gasp with relief to feel his pulse fluttering weakly beneath my fingertips.

If he was dead...

I can't tolerate the thought, not even for a millisecond. Quickly, I place a hand to the side of the stump of his severed tentacle, murmuring a spell under my breath.

The bleeding slows, but my body shakes hard with a chill as if from a fever.

I'm helping the ghosts and expending magical energy to help Ghastly too. Attempting to do both feels like trying to balance two cups of water on top of each other. I'm only going to end up losing one of them.

But I'm not on my own, either.

"Get Phineas!" I tell the ghosts, pointing. "There!"

The dead race over to him and break open the

door. Shifting back quickly from Beastly into his Jekyll form, Phineas stares like the door is possessed.

"Puck too," I call.

The Hyde is out the door the instant the dead break the locks. Both Phineas and Puck spare a fast look around like they can't see any of the ghosts helping us, but they only bother to worry about that for a moment before they're rushing across the room and past the bodies of the fallen traders to my side.

"We're going to get you out of here," I assure Ghastly.

Phineas arrives at the opening of the cage.

"Heal him," I beg as I move to the side to give Phineas space to reach into the cage. "Please."

He doesn't hesitate. Cupping a hand over the severed stump on Ghastly's back, he murmurs spells under his breath.

Relief floods through me as the wounds seal, the slow ooze of blood tapering off entirely. I carefully lift the tentacle where Zeb's arm would be and loop it over my shoulders, trying to lever him upright without causing him more pain.

Ghastly groans, but after a moment, several of his tentacles move to help push him away from the ground.

But he's so ashen. A sheen of cold sweat covers his

skin wherever it's not also coated in drying blood like black ink.

Phineas takes over when I emerge from the cage, hoisting Ghastly's tentacle and holding him upright.

Puck pulls me to him and nuzzles the top of my head. "Go home."

I nod and then look at the ghosts. "Thank you."

All around me, the dead smile as they fade into a light only I can see. The ghost girl is the last to leave. She waves to me like a little kid as she fades away, her voice so happy as she says, "Bye-bye."

Phineas and Puck are watching me when I look back at them. I don't know quite what to say, and now doesn't feel like the time. Not when we're still standing in the middle of a trader facility with dozens of their crew's corpses around us.

Strong shudders roll through Ghastly, and then he shifts back to Zeb's form. The Jekyll's face is haggard with pain and exhaustion, but he still manages a weak smile at me. "Hey, beautiful."

A sob catches in my throat, driven by relief and pain and fear, but I smile back while my eyes sting. "Hey."

He glances around at the destruction. "You all have a party without me?"

I choke on a laugh. "Not exactly."

"We'll explain later," Phineas says with a pointed look at me that definitely means I'm going to be the one doing the explaining. "We need to get out of here before any more of these bastards arrive."

That sobers Zeb up quickly. With Puck's arm around me and Phineas helping Zeb, we head for the door.

CHAPTER 17
MABEL

It takes almost two weeks before Zeb has recovered enough from his wounds and the blood loss to get around the guys' new apartment on his own, though it only took a few hours before he was tired of Huck and Phineas "hovering around him like mother birds."

Me, he never complains about. Well, never except to protest the fact I won't have sex with him while he's recovering.

I'm sitting next to Zeb in the bed, my back propped up on pillows, when the bedroom door opens and Phineas comes in. I've taken to sleeping in here ever since we arrived, usually with Huck spooned behind me and Phineas asleep on a cot near Zeb, just in case he needs help in the night. Creepy loves having all the men around us. She wouldn't have it any other way.

It hurts how much I like it too.

But soon, the time will come to move into my own place, even if that won't be my house. Though everything our contacts have found proves that when we broke out of the traders' facility we eliminated the last of the crew responsible for destroying my home, leaving no one who could know about us or about La Fleur's location, I still haven't been back to my house since that first day it burned. The insurance company has called a few times, and there's a chance they'll pay my claim if the arson investigator concludes the fire wasn't my fault. But given the amount of destruction, I'm not sure if what they give me will ever be enough to repair my home.

The reality of that is too painful to focus on, and until Zeb's better, there's only so much damage to the things I care about that I can stand at one time.

"Good morning," Phineas says.

Huck comes in behind him, a tray of food in his hands, and I can tell from the moment he sets it down that the Jekyll put it together himself. The pieces of toast are mildly burnt and the jam is melting off one side. The glasses of juice are so full, they've sloshed a bit onto the tray while he carried it. It's a far cry from the delicacies Zeb would whip up, but I love him for trying.

As I take a bite of the toast, Huck sinks down at my side, his fingers straying up and down my leg beneath the blankets, while Phineas takes a seat on the chair near the bed.

"If you're feeling up to it," Phineas says. "There's something we would like to ask you."

I think for a moment he's talking to Zeb, but then I realize he's looking at me. "Ask me what?"

Phineas glances at the others. "You said you didn't think this would work out. That our lives and yours weren't compatible."

I tense.

"The guys and I have been talking," Zeb says. "And we wondered if you wouldn't mind testing that theory."

I eye them warily. "What do you mean?"

"We travel," Phineas acknowledges. "Quite a bit, in all honesty. We go from one job to the next, day in and day out. And given the good that we can do, it doesn't seem advisable to us to stop."

I make myself nod, even if it hurts to hear everything I already know confirmed by him.

"But we've never had a home, either," Huck chimes

in. "I mean, they used to. I didn't. But now none of us do."

"Seems silly, really," Zeb adds.

"We could use a home base," Phineas says. "Somewhere to come back to when the traveling is done. And we thought perhaps New Orleans could be that place."

My brow twitches down. I know what I'm hoping, but I want them to speak the words out loud. I *need* them to because I don't want to be wrong about this. "What are you saying?"

Huck gives me a nervous smile. "Maybe we could make that home with you?"

I stare at them, my heart galloping in my chest and Creepy dancing for joy in my mind.

Zeb reaches over and takes my hand. "You run your business here. We travel as needed and then... come home. You get your space, we don't lose our work, and we all, you know"—he shrugs, that confident grin hovering around his lips—"live happily ever after."

My mouth moves for a moment before I can find words, while inside my head, Creepy bounces with excitement. "You'd do that?"

"Only if we can always come home to you." Zeb glances to the others. "Yeah?"

Huck nods eagerly. Phineas smiles.

I let out a shaky breath. "That... I don't know what to say. That'd be wonderful." Reality dims my happiness. "I guess we'll have to find a house. Or, you know, stay here or..."

I trail off, feeling conflicted. I don't want to be rude about the apartment they found after the traders broke into the last one. But like their previous place, this doesn't feel like a home. It's too sterile. Too much like a rich guy's vacation bachelor pad.

I can't imagine my clients feeling comfortable meeting me here, to say nothing of the lack of space for any of my associates from the underground who might pass through.

"Well," Huck says, smiling hopefully. "We were kind of thinking we could stay at your place."

"My... *burned* place?" My heart aches at having to acknowledge the damage.

"Only for now," Zeb says. At my confused look, he squeezes my hand. "You're not alone in this, Mabel. Whatever the insurance company does, we'll make sure you get your house back."

My mouth moves. "Thank you."

He nods. His hand doesn't leave mine, but suddenly a quivering feeling passes through his grip.

"In that case..." He grins. "I told you I had something special planned for you."

Now I'm confused again. "What are you—"

His arm shifts into a tentacle.

"No," I protest. "Zeb, no! You're still healing."

He sits up straighter in bed as tentacles emerge from his back as well. "I'm healed up enough, beautiful."

"And orgasms are quite beneficial for your health," Phineas adds.

I throw him an exasperated look. "Not helping."

The tentacle tightens on my hand, pulling my attention back. "I'm okay, Mabel. But if you really don't want to—"

"I didn't say that!"

At my blurted answer, Zeb grins again. "Then, as *I* was saying before we were so rudely interrupted weeks ago..." He pulls me out of bed. His grin stays even as he shifts, his eyes going white and his tentacles unfurling all around him, and suddenly Ghastly is looking back at me instead. "I planned something *special* for you."

The Hyde's voice is a dark and insidious murmur, like something from deep within a watery cave, and it sends a shiver down my spine that's equal parts fear and arousal. Though his arms are gone, his legs remain, and he steps closer to me in a sinuous movement that feels as much like he's dancing as walking.

"Puck," he says shortly.

I start to turn, but Ghastly's tentacles catch me. They slip beneath my shirt and undulate around my sides and up my spine. Another slithers around to the back of my neck and into my hair, keeping my head in position so I'm facing him.

My breath catches. Slowly, *agonizingly* slowly, the remainder of his tentacles begin removing my clothes, the first few holding me in place all the while. I bite my lip, staying still for him, my gaze locked on his milky-white eyes.

He's so alien, this Hyde, but even though I've only ever seen him briefly, there's still something so familiar about him too. Like something about me recognizes something about him, and not just because I have a Hyde too.

Because maybe we really are meant to be mates.

I smile as the last of my clothes fall away. "So what did you have in mind?"

Ghastly chuckles. He leans over a bit as if looking past me, though his white eyes make it hard to tell where he's looking at all. "Ready?"

Puck's hands slide around my sides. Ghastly's tentacles draw away as Puck turns me toward him.

I look between them, confused, but suddenly, Puck hoists me up, and on instinct, my legs wrap around his hips. He's holding me above his cock, the tip resting against my entrance but not entering me, and I wiggle against him, a needy sound escaping me.

"My greedy belle," Puck teases, but he doesn't lower me.

"One moment more," Ghastly tells me as his tentacles slide around me again. They slip along my back, along my legs, all over me.

Including between my legs.

I look down. The tip of one of his tentacles is wrapping around Puck's cock.

My confusion returns. "What are you—"

"Do you trust me, lovely?" Ghastly asks.

I don't need to think about it. I just nod.

He makes a pleased sound. The tentacles around my legs adjust to hold me wide open for them.

It suddenly occurs to me he's only been using the upper side of his tentacles, not the underside where the suckers reside. But before I can open my mouth to ask why, the tentacles suddenly rotate, the suckers gripping me on all sides while Puck pushes his tentacle-wrapped cock into me.

I gasp, tensing as suddenly my mind is flooded with awareness not just of Puck inside me, but of everything. Puck's hands and his chest and all of him that's touching me, so vivid it's as if I'm inside his skin.

His pleasure at filling me pounds through my head, making my soaked and needy pussy ache even more as his arousal mingles with mine.

Ghastly undulates his tentacles around me as he moves to one side, and I cry out. It's not just Puck I feel. Ghastly is part of this too. I feel every one of the suckers on his tentacles, not just *on* my skin, but how it is for him to be touching so much of me all at once.

"You doing okay?" he asks.

Breathless, I can only nod, my eyes wide as my body thrums with the arousal and pleasure pulsing through me from all sides.

"Let's get you nice and relaxed then," Ghastly says.

Puck slides in and out of me, and I cry out, overwhelmed by the flood of need and desire and pure sensation pounding through me. I rock my hips hard, meeting him, craving this like I've never craved anything in my life, and in only a moment, I'm already coming hard from the intense waves of pleasure frying my brain.

He doesn't stop. Doesn't come. Puck thrusts and thrusts in me while Ghastly's tentacles pulse across my skin, feeding me more sensation than I know how to handle.

I melt in their arms, and only his tentacles hold me upright. Over and over they wring orgasms from me, until my legs are wet with my own slick from how many times I've come in their grip.

And then Beastly steps into place behind me.

Puck stops moving inside me as one of Ghastly's tentacles slips away from my side.

I choke on a begging sound that turns into an incredulous whimper. Oh, gods, are they—

Surely not.

"Deep breath," Ghastly tells me.

Oh fuck.

Slowly, Beastly pushes into me too.

I cry out. Are they insane? There's no way this will work. "I-I can't. All of you are— I'm not—"

"My belle can do anything," Puck croons to me, adjusting his hips a bit while Beastly eases deeper into me and Ghastly's tentacles pulse around their cocks.

I quiver in their hands, barely daring to breathe while my body adjusts to the unbelievably full sensation of all three of them filling me. Even after all the orgasms they gave me, my pussy still aches at the way they're stretching me.

But it's an intensely delicious kind of pain. The kind that sends a rush of endorphins coursing through your blood because you've pushed past what you believed was possible, and now you feel exhilarated too.

And then they start moving.

A wild moan escapes me. Awareness of all three of my men's pleasure pours through my mind, sweeping me and Creepy away with it. Out of pure instinct, I rock between them too, all conscious thought abandoning me. My body turns to putty, obeying my desire for them and ignoring my incredulity at how it's even possible for them all to fit inside me.

I'm not a rational, sensible person anymore. I'm only my need. Only my craving for them and the fact I never want this to end. I move when they do, suspended between Ghastly's tentacles and Puck and Beastly's hands alike. My mind is lost to the tidal waves of sensation. I no longer recognize the sounds coming from me as I plead for them to continue, to never stop, to fuck me forever just like this because oh *gods...*

I scream as I come. My body goes rigid as ecstasy overtakes me, and I lose the room entirely as their orgasms take them too. I feel every second of it. Every rush of their pleasure. Every pulse of their cocks as they fill me with their cum. My release echoes it all, not stopping, pounding through me over and over like it'll never end. I swear it's an eternity until they're spent and I am too.

The world is soft and blurry, made of cotton and

light. I open my eyes to realize I'm back in the bed, which means I must have passed out from what we all did. But my Hydes are around me now, Puck tucked in close to me with Ghastly spooned behind him, his tentacles draped across us both, while Beastly is on my opposite side, supporting me with a furry arm under my head.

I smile sleepily. This is perfect.

Beastly notices I'm awake, and he grins his wolfish grin at me before shifting back to Phineas.

I nestle closer to my Jekyll's side.

"So what do you think, beautiful?" Zeb asks.

I glance back to see that he and Huck have shifted too.

Zeb smiles. "Will you give us a chance to be your mates forever?"

I nod, my heart feeling so warm and full, it's hard to find words. "Happily."

Three months later

"Now," Huck cautions. "Don't open your eyes, okay?"

Laughing, I walk carefully forward with my eyes closed. "Okay."

His grip on my hand tightens, bringing me to a stop. "Are you ready?" He doesn't sound like he's asking me.

"One more minute," Phineas replies.

"Come on, guys," I protest, keeping my eyes closed.

None of them responds for a moment. I hear shuffling feet and quick whispers back and forth.

"All right," Zeb says. "Open."

I open my eyes.

A tiny cry escapes me. We're standing on my street. My home is straight ahead of me. But no trace of the fire or even a smudge of soot remains on the brick walls or teal shutters. There are even flowers in planters by the front door.

"You like it?" Huck asks.

I press a hand to my lips as I nod. "It's perfect. But I thought the contractors said it'd be another two months before it was all fixed."

Zeb smiles. "We called in some help."

The front door swings open and I gasp a second time as Tamira grins at us. Weeks before, Zeb came clean on how he'd used Ghastly's powers on her that night when I ran from them at the bar. She'd been furious for a bit, but after plenty of promises that he'd never *dare* try it again, eventually she'd forgiven him.

After all, if anyone could understand the need to chase down their fleeing mate, it was a shifter.

Behind her, so many of my associates from the underground are waiting, smiles on their faces.

"Everybody helped on repairs," Tamira says. "We couldn't let you stay holed up in some bachelor pad forever."

I laugh while Phineas glowers.

"She has a point," Zeb says.

Phineas scoffs, but a smile twitches the corner of his lip.

"So what do you say?" Huck asks me. "Ready to go home?"

I lean into him as he puts his arm around me from one side and Zeb slides his around me from the other. "With you guys?" I say. "Always."

Want to see more of Mabel and her guys? Join Sierra Rowan's insider's club now at sierrarowan.com to be the first to hear about bonus scenes and new books where your favorite Jekylls and Hydes will make appearances!

TITLES BY SIERRA ROWAN

The Vampire Rebellion Series

Blood Pawn

Blood Captive

Blood Rebel

Blood Queen

Forever After: Crimson Snow

Of Snow So White

Of Blood So Red

Of Fate So Dark

Of Nine So Bold

Jekylls and Hydes

The Jekyll and Her Hydes

The Misfit and Her Monsters

ABOUT THE AUTHOR

Sierra Rowan is the USA Today bestselling author of action-packed reverse harem paranormal romance and urban fantasy novels. Sierra loves to write stories filled with steam, heart, and adventure where a happily-ever-after is guaranteed, even if it takes a few magical battles and wild escapes to get there.

Get updates about all of Sierra Rowan's books at sierrarowan.com.

amazon.com/author/sierrarowan
bookbub.com/authors/sierra-rowan
goodreads.com/sierrarowan